CHASING THE WIND

THE YOUNG UNDERGROUND

CHASING THE WIND

Robert Elmer

BETHANY HOUSE PUBLISHERS
MINNEAPOLIS, MINNESOTA 55438

Chasing the Wind
Copyright © 1996
Robert Elmer

Cover illustration by Chris Ellison

Published by Bethany House Publishers
A Ministry of Bethany Fellowship, Inc.
11300 Hampshire Avenue South
Minneapolis, Minnesota 55438

Printed in the United States of America.

Library of Congress Cataloging-in-Publication Data

Elmer, Robert.
    Chasing the wind / Robert Elmer.
        p. cm. — (The young underground ; #5)
    Summary: Just after the surrender of Germany in World War II, three
Danish children are trapped aboard a renegade German submarine
attempting to escape to South America with Nazi treasure.

    [1. Denmark—History—Fiction. 2. Buried treasure—Fiction.
3. Submarines—Fiction. 4. Christian life—Fiction.] I. Title. II. Series:
Elmer, Robert. Young underground ; #5.
    PZ7.E4794Ch   1996
    [Fic]—dc20   95–45104
    ISBN 1–55661–658–9   CIP
                                                                      AC

To my daughter, Danica Elise,
who has a servant's heart.

ROBERT ELMER has written and edited numerous articles for both newspapers and magazines in the Pacific Northwest. The YOUNG UNDERGROUND series was inspired by stories from Robert's Denmark-born parents, as well as friends who lived through the years of German occupation. He is currently a writer for an advertising agency in Bellingham, Washington. He and his wife, Ronda, have three children.

CONTENTS

Propellers and rudders

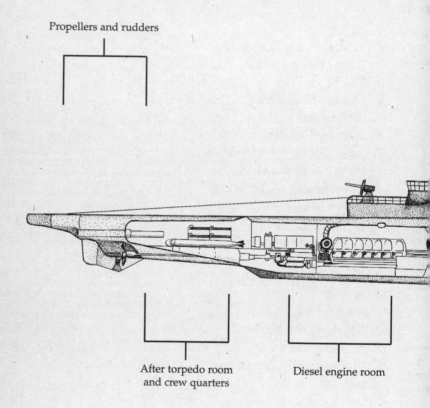

After torpedo room
and crew quarters

Diesel engine room

THE U-111

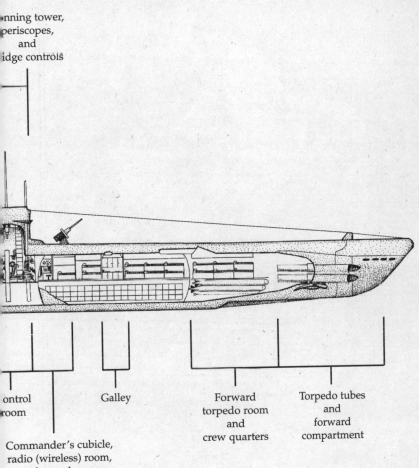

nning tower,
periscopes,
and
idge controls

ontrol
room

Galley

Forward
torpedo room
and
crew quarters

Torpedo tubes
and
forward
compartment

Commander's cubicle,
radio (wireless) room,
and sound room

Vulkan to the Rescue

June 1945

"You kids stay out of the way now," warned Captain Bering as he gripped the big wooden steering wheel of his tugboat. "We'll have that old ship pushed back into the harbor in just a few minutes."

The stocky, suntanned man looked more like a seagoing version of Santa Claus than a tugboat skipper. He squinted out into the bright fog, stroked his bushy white beard, and expertly eased his smaller boat into position next to the big, rusty-sided steamship.

Twelve-year-old Peter Andersen backed away from his spot next to his grandfather's friend and bumped into his twin sister, Elise, who was already almost three inches taller than Peter. They shared the same blond hair color and their father's steel-blue eyes. And both had the same slim build.

"Sorry," he told her, but Elise hardly noticed. Like the others, she was too interested in what was going on right next to the little tugboat.

Peter's best friend, Henrik Melchior, was stationed behind them in a corner of the wheelhouse. His dark eyes scanned the deck ten feet below, where two big-muscled deckhands wrestled with huge ropes descending from the ship the tugboat was going to push. When everything was ready, Captain Bering twisted the polished brass handles that controlled his boat's engines.

From somewhere below Peter, the tugboat *Vulkan* seemed to clear its throat. Peter felt the vibrations of its powerful twin engines right down to his bones. *This boat has the right name*, he thought. (Vulkan is Danish for volcano.) *Feels like the volcano's going to blow.*

Elise pushed her long hair away from her face, tapped on Peter's shoulder, and tried to tell him something as she pointed out the window.

"What did you say?" he shouted over the throaty roar of the engines.

"I said," she repeated into his ear, "the castle looks beautiful from here."

His sister was right. With its glittering green copper roofs and flags fluttering in the distance, Kronborg Castle looked like something out of a fairy tale as it peeked out through a hole in the fog. Behind the castle, the red tile roofs of their harbor city of Helsingor glittered in the early Saturday morning sunshine.

"Is it okay to go out on deck?" Elise asked the captain cautiously. He was concentrating on pushing the large ship, just as another tugboat was doing on the other side of the old freighter. The two tugboats worked as a team even though Captain Bering couldn't see what was happening on the other side. All they could see was the rusty metal of the big ship on the one side, and the open harbor with the castle and city in the background on the other. Then thick tendrils of fog began to close in around the ship.

For a minute, the captain said nothing, as if he was thinking. He leaned forward on the wheel and looked up at the rusty ship. The two boats rose and fell together on gentle ocean swells.

"Fine, you can go on deck," he finally replied. "Just watch out for Carlsen. He doesn't like kids, and I promised your grandfather I'd take care of you."

"We'll be careful," Peter assured him.

"Yeah," echoed Henrik, his dark hair looking wild in the wind. "Don't worry about us."

It was the first time since the war had ended that they had seen Helsingor from the water, and Peter wanted to see more. And besides, he told himself, it would be the perfect way to get their minds off school. At least, that's how he and Henrik had convinced Elise to come along. Monday would be the start of their last week of classes and all the end-of the year tests. But Monday was still two days away. The three of them climbed down the little ladder down to the deck.

"Watch for sailboats coming out of the fog." Elise pointed in the direction of Helsingor's yacht harbor. "People are starting to put their boats in the water again."

Peter nodded and breathed in the damp, salty air—absolutely his favorite smell. *Nothing is better than being out on the water like this*, he thought to himself. *Absolutely nothing.* He looked around in satisfaction at the large tug, then waved up to Captain Bering above them in the wheelhouse. His grandfather's friend waved and nodded down at the trio and blasted on his big foghorn.

The twins jumped, then looked at each other and smiled. Henrik put his fingers in his ears and grinned, too.

"Pretty loud," he said, looking out into the fog. Then he froze and grabbed Peter's arm. "What was that?"

Peter felt rather than heard the boom, even over the vibrations and noise of the old tugboat. Elise stared out into the fog.

"Sounded like a cannon shot, only different," said Peter, looking up to see if Captain Bering had noticed.

"Is that where it came from?" he asked, pointing off to the right. Henrik shrugged.

"I think it was over to the left," suggested Elise.

"Look—out there to the right!" she pointed. Peter strained to see through the light-gray fog. He thought he spotted some wreckage floating on the water.

"I see it, too," echoed Henrik. "It's a boat—or part of one."

Peter quickly led the way, with Henrik close behind him, back up the stairway to where Captain Bering was steering.

"I see it," Captain Bering told them when they burst into the wheelhouse. He slowed down the *Vulkan's* speed. "Any closer, and we'd run right over it."

"What happened?" asked Peter.

"Explosion—I don't really know," answered the captain, not taking his eyes off what was plainly now a pile of wreckage. They could just see the hull of a medium-sized metal boat, twisted like a pretzel and turned turtle in the still ocean.

One thing's sure, thought Peter. *It didn't turn over because the weather was too rough.*

"I see a man!" Elise pointed. "He's hanging on to the hull."

"You kids stay up here," ordered the captain. "I don't want you getting hurt."

The twins and Henrik stood watch in the wheelhouse as the two deckhands threw a rope overboard and fished the unlucky man from the wreckage. They rolled him up and over the railing of the tugboat and helped him to his feet.

The survivor was a large, square-shouldered man. His black beard had a distinctive silver streak down the middle—almost like a skunk's. He stood motionless on the deck, dripping and watching the twisted piece of metal that was his boat flip before disappearing into a boil of bubbles and foam. Then the man clenched his fists and looked over his shoulder and up at the twins, who were watching from beside Captain Bering. For a moment, the wild-looking man stared straight at Peter, as if it were all his fault. Peter shivered and looked away.

"We picked that fellow up not a moment too soon," murmured the captain. Then he leaned out his door and bellowed down at his crew.

"Don't just stand there looking at the man. Bring him up here."

Still dripping, the man climbed the ladder and swung into the wheelhouse. Peter, Elise, and Henrik quickly backed into a corner to make room.

"Thank you, Captain," boomed the man. Peter thought his Danish betrayed an accent, but he wasn't quite sure. One thing was sure, however: the man with the skunk beard was used to ordering people around. He practically pushed Captain Bering away from the wheel.

"Excuse me, Captain, but I must know where we are. Let me check a couple of compass bearings, and I'll be out of your way."

Captain Bering's eyes grew wide, and he puffed his cheeks impatiently, but he stepped back for a moment as the man checked the tugboat's compass against a couple of landmarks. The tips of the Kronbörg Castle's towers were just peeking out of the fog.

"What's he doing?" whispered Henrik.

"Shh!" answered Elise. "For some reason, he's trying to see where we are."

"But everyone knows where we are," protested Henrik. "The castle's right over there, behind all that fog."

"I think he wants to know exactly."

Peter didn't take his eyes off the soaked man. Neither did Captain Bering, who had his hands on his hips and was looking impatiently at the back of the man's head.

"Now, see here," Captain Bering finally protested. "You're welcome to dry off in my cabin, but I have a ship to bring in."

The man ignored Captain Bering for a moment, checked the compass again, then straightened out and turned around with what looked like a make-believe smile. Except for a glimmer of gold on a top front tooth, his teeth were pearly and straight, and he stared aristocratically down his long, straight beak of a nose at the captain.

"Thank you, my friend," he told Captain Bering, ignoring the kids. "I have what I need. Do you have a dry towel ready in my—ah . . . your cabin?"

"Hanging by the bunk," replied Captain Bering, taking the

wheel. "The cabin is outside and right below us."

The man nodded and was gone.

"Wow, you'd think he owned the boat, or something," whispered Henrik. "Where do you think he was from?"

But no one had a chance to wonder. Just then, a muffled explosion burst from behind and beneath them, and a column of water rained high over their heads. The back end of the tugboat picked up like a wild horse and threw Henrik and Elise roughly to the floorboards. Peter grabbed the side of the door to hold himself up.

"What's going on?" shouted Henrik as he and Elise scrambled to their feet.

Peter could only think they were under attack. With his heart racing wildly, he scanned the ocean around them. The tugboats and the old ship were the only boats in the area, as far as he could tell. And the explosion—or whatever it was—had knocked their tugboat away from the rusty freighter.

Captain Bering was still on his feet. "Tighten those lines!" he shouted, and his deckhands flew into action on the forward deck of the tug. The man with the skunk beard had already disappeared into the captain's room below.

Above them, excited faces appeared over the railing of the big ship. But they could only watch as the *Vulkan* strained against its side, this time at full power.

"Was the explosion on the *Vulkan*?" asked Elise.

"Incompetents!" fumed the captain. "I asked the British minesweepers if all the mines had been cleared out of this area." He was sweating, and the veins in his neck were bulging. "I must have asked them ten times if all the mines were clear. And ten times they said yes!"

"Did we hit a mine?" Henrik's eyes were wide.

"Not us," answered Captain Bering. He pointed up behind them at a gaping hole near the freighter's waterline. What was left of the ship's huge propeller was mangled and twisted, hanging by only a few shreds of metal.

"Magnetic mine," the captain finally replied. "The British planted a few here a couple of years ago, but they were supposed to have retrieved them all. This is the first one I've ever seen." He looked back for a moment at the hole in the other ship. Water was pouring in, but most of the damage was to the propeller and rudder.

"Make that the second one," added the captain. "Our passenger probably found the first with his little boat."

"Is the freighter going to sink, too?" asked Elise. "It's getting lower in the water."

The captain shook his head and quickly grabbed a microphone from his old radio overhead. He flipped a switch and waited a moment for it to warm up.

"They won't sink as long as they start pumping water out of their ship right away," he reassured Elise. "They're lucky. Very lucky. Wasn't much of a mine. In fact, I don't think it exploded quite the way it was supposed to. Acted almost like a dud."

"Could have fooled me," mumbled Henrik, still holding on for dear life to a side railing by the door.

"Helsingor harbor master," Captain Bering boomed into the microphone. Peter wondered if the radio was really necessary, the captain's voice was so loud. "This is the tug *Vulkan*. Are you there?"

The radio only hissed and sputtered in return.

As the captain repeated his call, a spout of water came pouring down at them from the ship above, soaking one of the young deckhands standing at the front of their boat. The men high above them were starting to pump the water out of their sinking ship—but it was pouring like a waterfall right down on top of the *Vulkan*!

"Hey!" yelled Captain Bering out his window. "Aim to the side! We're down here!"

But no one on the big ship seemed to hear. They just kept pumping water from their sinking ship, without realizing where it was going. The man up front was facedown on the tugboat deck, knocked down by a giant stream of water.

Captain Bering didn't waste a second. He dropped his micro-phone and pulled Peter by the shoulder until he stood in front of the wheel.

"Right there," he instructed. "Just keep it steady. Under-stand?"

Peter nodded and grabbed the spokes of the steering wheel. He could hardly see over the top, but he was determined to keep the boat on course for the harbor. After all, he had steered his uncle's fishing boat before.

Captain Bering flew down the left side ladder like a fireman down a pole to reach his injured crewman. As Peter, Elise, and Henrik watched helplessly, he pulled the young man out of the waterfall to a safer part of the deck.

Henrik craned his neck to watch the scene of the rescue.

"Is he all right?" asked Elise.

"He's sitting up and coughing," Henrik reported. "But all this water's going to sink us. Don't they know what they're doing up there?"

Peter looked up but saw nothing. He jumped when he heard a loud voice.

"Helsingor harbor master here, go ahead."

Captain Bering was still huddled over the injured crewman, who was slumped against the side of the wheelhouse. Water ran like a river down the side deck and out the back.

"This is the Helsingor harbor master," announced the radio for the second time. "Bering, are you there? Over."

Elise reached over and picked up the dangling microphone. She squeezed the switch on the side of it and spoke so softly that Peter could hardly hear her.

"Um . . . this isn't Captain Bering. This is Elise Andersen. The captain had to leave the wheelhouse because one of his crewmen was injured."

The radio crackled and hissed once more, and Elise squeezed the switch. "Over."

"Come again? Is this the *Vulkan*? Who is this? Over."

Henrik put out his hand to take the microphone. "Here, let me talk to him," he commanded.

But Elise swung away and tried again in a louder voice.

"This is the *Vulkan*," she said, this time much louder. "Captain Bering can't come to the phone—I mean the radio. We're about ten minutes from the harbor, but the ship we were pushing has a big hole in it, and I think Captain Bering wanted to warn you we were coming in with a sinking ship. Over."

There was another short silence, then the harbor master spoke up once more. "Okay, I understand. Do you need some help out there? Over."

"Yes—at least, I think so. Maybe you can tell us where to put this ship before it sinks."

"All right, *Vulkan*, we don't want you to drop this load in the mouth of the harbor. We'll be right there."

Elise hung the microphone carefully on its hook but left the radio on. A few minutes later, a dripping Captain Bering burst back into the wheelhouse and patted Peter on the shoulder.

"Good job, skipper. You did just fine, but I better take it from here."

Henrik leaned out the door. "Is he okay?"

"He's fine," replied the captain. "Hit his head hard on something when he was knocked to the deck, though. He'll probably need a couple of stitches back by his ear." He pointed behind his right ear. "But all in all, he's fine—" He stopped abruptly as he glanced up at the railing of the ship, caught sight of someone, and gestured wildly for them to direct the shower of water elsewhere. Finally, a man in a black officer's cap smiled and waved down at them.

Captain Bering returned the salute but didn't smile.

"If they were paying attention in the first place, they would have saved us a lot of headaches," mumbled the captain between his teeth. But by then the twin tugs, *Vulkan* and *Aktiv*, were making progress toward the harbor entrance. Peter was glad they weren't far away.

"Almost there," observed Elise. She and the boys kept looking back and forth between the hole in the ship they were pushing and the harbor light standing at the end of the long, concrete finger pier that protected their harbor.

"Are you sure it's not sinking?" asked Peter.

"Nothing's going to sink," the captain assured them. But his voice didn't sound as sure as before.

Several people had gathered by the little white lighthouse at the harbor entrance to watch as the two tugboats came in closer with the crippled freighter. A little girl waved. A moment later, a small, gray Danish coastal patrol boat raced out of the harbor to meet them. The tug's radio crackled to life once more.

"*Vulkan*, how are you doing there? Is the captain still taking a nap?"

Captain Bering grabbed the microphone. "Who's taking a nap? My tow took a hit from a mine. Over."

"Bering, why don't you just lean out the window and holler at me? I could probably hear you just as well. Over."

"Look, young fellow, I don't have time to chat. I'm looking for a place to park. And we're in a hurry, if you don't mind."

"Right," answered the voice. It sounded like the same man Elise had talked with a minute earlier. "Your granddaughter told me that already. Follow me inside."

Captain Bering glanced sideways at Elise and winked. "Pretty good crew I've picked up here. A helmsman and a radio operator. And now I seem to have a new granddaughter, too."

The patrol boat made a U-turn and pointed the way through the opening to the harbor, about as far away as two or three football fields. They hurried past a line of ships and ferries, making their way to the closest open shipyard dock. A shipyard crane was quickly being pulled into place as a crowd of workers scattered to make room along the pier.

"Wow!" grinned Henrik as their tugboat nudged the big ship

up to the pier. "I thought we were just going out for a Saturday morning ride."

But Captain Bering was too busy concentrating on keeping his side of the ship in place to respond. After a few more minutes of pushing and pulling and making sure workers had the crippled ship in place, he finally relaxed.

"Look, kids, I'm sorry." The captain pulled at his belt and reached over to turn off the tugboat's engines. "If I would have known what kind of ride that was going to be, I would never have let you out with me."

"It wasn't your fault," replied Elise, taking a deep breath and leaning against the wall. Peter thought her face looked pale.

"You said you checked first to make sure it was safe," added Henrik.

"At least ten times." The older man frowned as he looked at the crew of shipyard workers swarming over the freighter. "And I've been out on these waters every day for the past five years of the war without running into any of the problems we ran into today. I'm going to give those British minesweeper people a piece of my mind. They told me it was completely safe, or I would never have let you kids tag along."

Peter gave his sister a concerned look. He was shaking a little, too. "It's okay, Captain Bering. Really. We're fine."

"Yeah," added Henrik. "We won't tell Peter's parents about this."

"Henrik," scolded Elise. "We will, too."

"Now, what about that guy we picked up?" asked Henrik.

Peter looked out the door of the *Vulkan*'s wheelhouse and down at the deck, where one of the deckhands was cleaning up.

"Where did that fellow go?" yelled Captain Bering.

The injured deckhand popped out of the captain's room and onto the deck. "That man we picked up isn't inside your cabin, Captain," he reported. "Must have jumped to shore as soon as we pulled up."

"You mean he disappeared?" asked Henrik, swinging down the ladder to the deck.

Peter looked out the window to see his grandfather hurrying across the pier toward the tugboat. Peter almost fell as he waved out the door of the wheelhouse.

"Grandfather!" he yelled. "You'll never guess what happened!"

2

RUMORS OF TREASURE

"I'm sorry, Arne," Grandfather Andersen apologized for the third time. Peter didn't like to see his grandfather's usually bright eyes so full of worry. "I had no idea something like that could happen. If I had, I would never have let my friend Bering take the kids out."

The Andersens were finishing their dinner. Mrs. Andersen put her hand on her father-in-law's arm and tried to smile. She brushed her pretty red hair away from her forehead, her eyebrows wrinkled in concern. "Dad, we're not blaming you," she said. "We've talked with the harbor patrol, and they said the same thing. No one had any idea there were mines still out there. It was just one of those things—"

"Yes," Grandfather interrupted, "but I still feel very responsible."

Mrs. Andersen shook her head. "How could you have known? How could anyone have known?"

"But I was the one who talked Bering into it," continued Grandfather. He put his cloth napkin down next to his plate, ran his fingers through his thinning silver hair, and crossed his arms. "They could have been hurt."

Mr. Andersen pushed his chair out slowly and unfolded his tall legs from under the table. When his father stood up that way, slowly and carefully, Peter knew some kind of speech was coming.

"The kids weren't any trouble from what I understand," said Mr. Andersen, clearing his throat with a deep rumble. Then he looked seriously at Peter and Elise. It was not the sort of look Peter could avoid.

"In fact," he continued, "Bering said he was awfully glad to have them along."

"He was?" said Peter, choking on his last mouthful of cucumber salad.

Even Elise put down her fork in surprise. "What did Captain Bering say?"

"He just told me that I should be proud to have three kids who behave so well during a tough situation. And, Henrik, I hope you don't mind being included in that number. Since you've been with us over the past six weeks, well, it seems like you've become a part of the family."

Henrik nodded politely and lowered his eyes. He had been staying since May with the Andersen family while his father recovered from a heart attack in Sweden.

"The point is," finished Mr. Andersen, "we're proud of you three for doing the right thing, for helping Captain Bering."

"Does that mean we don't have to do the dishes tonight?" ventured Peter.

Mrs. Andersen looked at her husband and burst out laughing. "Spoken like a true twelve-year-old," she said as she stacked the dinner dishes. "But no, it's dishes as usual. Whose turn is it?"

"Elise's," Peter blurted out just as Henrik said, "Peter's."

"No," Elise corrected them. "It's Saturday night, remember? It's your turn, boys."

"I think you're right, Miss Andersen," said Peter's father as he slipped out of the kitchen and settled into his favorite over-stuffed chair in the living room. He picked up the evening news-paper, shuffled a few pages, and turned to Grandfather Andersen, who had joined him.

"Dad, you didn't happen to pick up the front page section, did you?"

"No, Arne," Grandfather replied.

"That was me, Mr Andersen," Henrik said from where he scrubbed the dishes Peter brought to the sink. "I'll get it right back to you."

"Oh, there's no hurry, Henrik. Whenever you've read it."

Henrik turned to Peter with a sly grin. "Want to hear what I figured out?"

Peter raised his eyebrows.

"Here, I'll show you." Henrik stepped away from the sink for a moment and returned from the room with a section of news-paper. "Here, Elise." He handed her the paper. "Can you read it while we finish up the dishes?"

As Henrik returned to the suds, Elise skimmed the headlines. " 'United Nations Formed in San Francisco,' 'New Polish Government . . .' "

Henrik waved a plate. "Look at the bottom of the page."

" 'Europe's Greatest Art Treasures Recovered'?"

"Yeah, that's it! Read it."

"Okay," Elise finally agreed, a little reluctantly. " 'American troops near Salzburg, Austria, have uncovered an incredible collection of Europe's most valuable art and cultural treasures in the Alt Aussee salt mines. The treasures were stolen by the Nazis from collections and governments all across the Continent during the war.' "

"You're getting to the good part," Henrik urged her on.

" 'But according to records found at the site, several treasures are missing, including the crown jewels of Czechoslovakia, ancient swords and shields, and five boxes of priceless gold coins.' "

"So let me get this straight," said Peter. "The Nazis stole crown jewels and stuff whenever they took over a country."

Henrik nodded and flicked a handful of suds at Peter. "You've got it. But read the last part, Elise."

Elise cleared her throat. " 'Gold items worth ten million dollars were removed from the collection by a Dr. Rudolph Wolffhardt only two weeks before the end of the war. Wolffhardt was last reported in the German port city of Kiel three days before the German surrender in May. Authorities have been unable to locate him or the remainder of the missing Nazi treasure since then, and many believe he may have tried to escape by sea.' "

"Wow," said Peter. "That means he would come by Helsingor."

"Exactly," agreed Henrik, pointing in the direction of the harbor.

Elise started giggling and put the paper down on the kitchen table. "You're nutty, Henrik Melchior. You too, Peter. You're both silly."

Henrik looked hurt. "Well, I didn't say I knew how to find the treasure. But just think of what you could do with all that money!"

"Right." Elise picked up a towel and dried off a pot. "You could start by hiring a maid to do your dishes."

3

THE BLACK BOAT

"Wouldn't it be nice to find some treasure," Peter whispered to himself as he dressed Sunday morning. He picked up an aluminum-colored two-penny piece and imagined for a minute that it was a handful of gold coins.

"What'd you say?" asked Henrik from his bed.

"Nothing," answered Peter, pulling on his best white shirt. He glanced over at his alarm clock to see how much time they had before Grandfather Andersen would stop by to pick him and Elise up for church.

"Come on, Peter, we're going to be late," called Elise from the hallway.

"I'm coming, I'm coming."

But by the time he made it to the kitchen, Elise was already finishing her cheese and bread. She looked up and grinned at him.

"A little slow today, sleepyhead?"

Peter didn't answer, just sat down and poured himself a glass of milk. "Pass the bread, would you?"

"Would I what?"

"Would you, please?"

Elise passed the French bread. Suddenly, there was a knock at the front door.

"It's Grandfather." She jumped up to get the door.

"Ready to go?" asked Grandfather Andersen from the street. "Church starts in ten minutes. We're late."

Peter poked his head back into his room before he ran down the stairs. "See you after church?"

"I'll be here," replied Henrik.

That had become their usual Sunday routine. Peter and Elise left with Grandfather Andersen to go to church, while Henrik and Peter's parents stayed home. Peter paused for a moment outside his parents' bedroom door, wanting to knock. It had never bothered him before that his parents didn't go to church, but lately . . .

"Peter?" called his sister.

"Coming."

Peter stopped by the kitchen table once more, stuffing another slice of bread into his pants pocket. Then he was out the door, slamming it behind him.

"All set?" asked his grandfather, still waiting at the bottom of the stairs. Peter nodded, and Grandfather looked past him, the way he often did, his eyebrows arched hopefully.

"No one else is coming, Grandfather," Peter told him.

"Ah well." Grandfather Andersen adjusted his thin black tie, the only one he owned. "I've been praying for that son of mine for a long time. So we'll keep praying for your parents, won't we? And for Henrik, too."

Peter swallowed, closed his eyes, and nodded again. He had never been able to figure out why his mom and dad didn't want to go to the little church Grandfather Andersen and their Uncle Morten attended most Sundays.

"When will Uncle Morten be home, Grandfather?" asked Peter, changing the subject.

Grandfather Andersen stopped for a moment to catch his breath. He seemed to have to do that more often lately.

"He didn't say, exactly." Grandfather leaned on Elise for balance. "But the honeymooners have been gone for a week or two now, haven't they?"

"Two weeks," answered Elise.

"Hmm, yes." Grandfather nodded and smiled. "And now how about you two? Are you both ready for your final exams?"

"We're ready," answered Elise. "We've been studying math together. Even Peter knows it pretty well."

"And how about Henrik? How is he managing?" Grandfather went on.

"Oh, he's okay. Just a little wild and crazy," answered Peter.

"He likes to give that impression, doesn't he?" Grandfather looked thoughtful. "Has he heard anything about his father lately?"

Peter had to think for a moment. "I heard Henrik talking on the phone with his mom the other day, and he sounded really worried and serious. But when I try to ask him about it, he acts as if everything's great."

Grandfather rested for a moment. "That sounds like Henrik."

"But right now all he talks about is the missing Nazi treasure," put in Elise.

Peter walked backward for a few steps. "Yeah, he'd really like to discover it and get rich."

Grandfather chuckled. "Sounds as though he's chasing the wind."

Peter looked at his grandfather. He wasn't sure he understood.

"I'm sorry, Peter. I overheard you three talking last night about the treasure, and it reminded me of what Solomon said in the Bible. Something like, 'Sinners spend their time gathering money, but then they lose it all again.' He goes on to say it's meaningless—like chasing the wind."

"Chasing the wind," echoed Peter. He jingled the two small coins in his pocket and imagined again that they were part of the missing treasure.

———

"So who's going with me to the castle?" asked Henrik later that Sunday afternoon.

"The castle? What for?" Peter looked up from the newspaper he had spread all over the floor.

Henrik shrugged. "No reason. Just for fun."

Elise looked up from her book, slipped a bookmark in her place, and got up. "I'm going to fall asleep if we don't go somewhere. Just let me get my shoes on."

"I'll get Dad's binoculars," volunteered Peter, heading for the hall closet.

A few minutes later, they were headed down Axeltorv Street on their bicycles, winding through the old part of town with its narrow cobblestone streets, and then on to busy King Street and Kronborg Castle on the edge of town. Halfway there, Peter knew his rope tires weren't going to last another block.

"Hey, slow down!" he called to Henrik and Elise, who were out ahead.

The rope his father had wrapped tightly around the rim of his wheel was flapping wildly, coming apart in the middle of an intersection.

"Worthless wheel," Peter mumbled, getting off his bike. He pushed through the intersection, ignoring the pieces of rope that had flown off on the road behind him. He took another look at the worn-out bicycle and shoved it in disgust to the ground. Then he gave it a kick for good measure—and stubbed his front toe hard as he caught his foot in the spokes.

"Ow!" he cried, falling to the sidewalk. But instead of getting up, he just sat there, staring at his broken bicycle.

"What are you doing down there?" he heard his sister ask him.

"I thought the war was over," he told Elise in disgust. "Aren't we supposed to have real tires again?"

Elise shrugged and shook her head. "Why don't you just park

it here in front of that store? We'll pick it up on the way back."

"Sounds good to me," agreed Peter, dusting himself off. "Maybe someone will steal it, and then I can get a new one."

"You don't need a new bike," Elise told him, getting off her own bicycle and walking beside him down the street to where Henrik was waiting. "Just a new tire."

Peter pretended not to hear her. *It wouldn't take much Nazi treasure to buy a new bike,* he told himself.

Kronborg Castle was already in sight at the end of the street, just around the north side of the harbor. Peter ran the last block, holding on to the fender of Elise's bike to keep up with her.

"To the north tower," shouted Henrik, leaving his bicycle outside the tall castle walls. The building was shaped like a square, ringed by tall walls that surrounded a huge courtyard. Two corners were crowned by tall observation towers, one by a smaller guard tower. The fourth corner was a squared-off room no taller than the green copper roofs that topped the castle.

Peter had seen plenty of pictures of castles in places like Germany and France, even castles in other parts of Denmark. But to his eye, Kronborg was the grandest. And with the end of the war, red-and-white Danish flags seemed to flutter everywhere. It was a wonderful change from the Nazi banners that had dotted their city during the war.

Kronborg was also the best place anywhere to explore. Henrik led the other two in a sprint across the central courtyard to the entrance of the north tower, the one closest to the ocean. By then, Peter had forgotten all about his broken bike.

"Don't forget, I have the binoculars," Peter shouted up the dark spiral stairway where Henrik had disappeared.

Counting the stairs, Peter lost track just before one hundred. A minute later, he and Elise stepped out into the tower balcony and blinked their eyes at the view. He had seen it a hundred times, but Peter always caught his breath at the sight. From here, they could see straight across the water to Sweden, or back across the courtyard and beyond that to the red roofs of their city. Peter handed the binoculars to Elise.

"I see the ship that almost sank," he said, turning his back on the ocean and pointing over toward the harbor. "There's the *Vulkan*, too, still tied up where Captain Bering left it."

"Yeah," said Henrik, his eyes following Peter's pointing finger. Even the roof of Grandfather Andersen's boathouse, off at the other side of the harbor, was clearly visible.

"Boys, you might want to see this," said Elise, scanning the water with the field glasses. "It's a really ugly old boat. Kind of like a fishing boat painted black."

"Oh." Henrik sounded disappointed. "I thought you found something."

"I did." Elise lowered the binoculars for a moment to get a view of the entire sound. Then she looked through them again. "They're going back and forth over that same area where we were yesterday—the place where the boats hit the mines."

"Are you sure?" Peter could barely make out the outline of the trawler Elise was watching in the distance.

"I think so. It's a dark, dirty-looking boat. Doesn't have Danish numbers on the front."

"See anyone on it?" Henrik's voice raised a notch.

"Take a look," said Elise, passing the binoculars to Henrik. "They're dragging something in the water, and they have lots of equipment on deck."

"Lots of fishing boats have stuff on deck," countered Peter.

"This isn't a fishing boat," announced Henrik, taking a long look through the glasses. "I see it, too."

"See what?" Without the binoculars, Peter couldn't notice anything unusual about the boat. Straining his eyes, he leaned over the stone railing. He couldn't quite tell, but the boat they were looking at seemed only a little larger than his uncle's fishing boat, the *Anna Marie*.

"Here." Henrik handed him the binoculars. "See for yourself."

Through his father's powerful binoculars, Peter could make

out two men on the cluttered deck. One was turning the handle on some kind of crank suspended over the back of the boat, while the other was leaning out, holding a rope. Around them was a strange pile of equipment, most of it covered by dark tarps. Only one contraption was uncovered, and it looked like a large red air tank with metal-spoked wheels on either side.

"Looks like they're pulling something up with the rope." Peter wasn't sure.

"What's happening?" asked Elise.

"The man at the crank just stopped to help pull something into their boat," Peter reported. "Looks like a big . . . I can't tell what it is."

"What do you mean, you can't tell?" Henrik was hopping up and down.

"It looks like a piece of junk. Now they're throwing it back into the water."

"And now they're going back and forth again," Elise observed, taking another turn at the binoculars. "Wait! It looks like one of the men has a beard just like the man we picked up yesterday."

"Let me see," said Henrik, taking the binoculars. "What would he be doing out there?"

"Isn't it obvious?" Elise looked at him. "Remember how worried he was about making sure he knew exactly where his boat sank? They're trying to salvage it."

"Yeah, but why would they do that?" Henrik focused the binoculars for a better view. "From what I saw, it didn't seem like there was much of a boat left to save."

Elise nodded. "Maybe not. But maybe there's something inside that boat that they really want."

The Boat Builders

"This is going to be great," said Henrik. He was down on his knees under Grandfather Andersen's rowboat, the same one they had used for years. "We'll make this into a real sailboat in no time. Here, you two, help me turn this over."

"Um . . . I think I have to study for my math exam," said Elise, looking at the boat. It had been stored under a tarp against the side of the boathouse for the last month.

"But we've been studying for weeks," replied Henrik, looking up. "You know it all by heart."

"Geography, then," Elise tried once more. "We'll have to know all the parts of the compass, all the countries in Africa, and—"

"Come on, Elise," replied Henrik, taking hold of the side of the boat. "That test isn't until Friday morning, and it's still Monday. We need some help today."

Peter looked at his sister and raised his eyebrows in question. She sighed and put down her school books. "All right," she told them. "But only for an hour. Then I have to do some more studying. You should, too."

"We could start studying out here." Henrik always had an answer. "You could draw a map of the harbor, and . . . uh . . . maybe that would help you remember your geography terms." He grinned at Elise.

"Hey, that's a pretty good idea," said Peter, taking the other end of the upside-down boat. "I think I'll do that, too."

The three of them gently rolled the boat over and stood back to look. All around them, the harbor buzzed with the usual work sounds of saws and motors, cranes and boat whistles.

"We still have to ask Grandfather if it's all right to turn it into a sailboat," warned Elise.

"That won't be a problem," replied Henrik, pulling out a piece of paper from his shirt pocket. "I have it all figured out. We won't have to drill any holes or change it much."

"Let's see," said Peter. For the moment, he forgot all about the math test. They were building a sailboat!

"What's this?" came Grandfather's voice from behind them a few minute later. "Carpenters?"

Elise was inside the boathouse looking for something to use for a sail while the boys were setting up sawhorses for a piece of plywood they had found under the shed.

"Oh, hi, Grandfather," replied Peter. "We were waiting for you to show up. Is it okay to use this piece of wood?"

"That piece?" Grandfather Andersen put on his glasses and took a closer look. "Plywood. Of course. But what's it for?"

"That's our other question." It was Henrik's turn to ask. "We were hoping that since no one is using that little rowboat—well, don't you think it would make a perfect sailboat?"

"You're saying you want to turn it into a sailboat?"

The boys nodded, and Grandfather scratched his chin.

"The harbor patrolmen said there aren't any other mines," Henrik eagerly pointed out. "And even if there were, the mines would be magnetic, so they wouldn't stick to our wood boat. And—"

"You're going to make a great salesman someday, Henrik," interrupted Grandfather. "Just so you don't go sailing off to Sweden this time. Try to stay in the harbor at first."

Peter smiled. "Thanks, Grandfather! We'll be careful."

Grandfather bent down closer to the drawing they were making. "Very good. Only the leeboard needs to dip down more, like this."

Henrik and Peter watched while Grandfather Andersen made another sketch—about two feet long and shaped like a fat peanut—on the sheet of plywood.

"There," finished Grandfather. "That's about the right shape. Now, you'll need to bolt it to the side of the boat so the end pokes straight down into the water."

"But what's it do?" asked Henrik.

"It gives us a way to steer the boat," said Elise from behind an armload of canvas.

Grandfather looked from the boys to Elise. "Looks like we have a skipper already, don't we, boys?"

————

The next day after school, they raced one another to the harbor. Henrik was eager to finish their rudder and the steering stick attached to it.

It was Elise's job to cut out and sew the sail. She laid the canvas out on the concrete of the boatyard next to the shed as she made neat seams with a needle and thread.

"Trapezoid." She held up the fabric and quizzed the boys. "What's a trapezoid?"

"A quadrilateral plane with two parallel sides," answered Henrik. "Same shape as our sail."

"How'd you know that?" Peter asked him, amazed that his friend had come up with the right answer so quickly.

"We studied for the math and geometry test last night after you fell asleep." Henrik smiled his widest smile.

"Don't worry, we'll study it again tonight," said Elise, holding up a corner of the white canvas where she had sewn on a small Danish flag.

"At least I know that shape," said Peter with a smile. "The flag is a rectangle."

Henrik grinned and gave him a thumbs-up sign.

"Think we'll be finished by Saturday?" Peter asked, dabbing some more white paint on his leeboard.

"Absolutely," Henrik answered. "Our first sail will be Saturday morning, if skipper Elise is ready."

"Who, me?" Elise looked up from her sewing for a moment. "I thought you were going to steer, Henrik. I can work the sail."

"Fine with me."

Peter looked at the leeboard he was working on thoughtfully, wondering how he'd gotten stuck in the middle. "I guess I'll be in charge of the leeboard."

––––––––––

The only thing Peter didn't like about working after school every day was that they ended up doing their studying late at night.

"Seems as though my brain turns to cheese after eight o'clock," Peter told Henrik, who was lying on the floor doing push-ups, a book in front of his nose. Peter was stretched out on the bed, finishing up a list of geography definitions for their last test.

"Is the Tropic of Cancer in the Northern Hemisphere, and the Tropic of Capricorn in the Southern?" asked Peter. "I always get those two mixed up."

Henrik squinted up at Peter and kept counting his push-ups. "Thirteen, fourteen. Cancer, Northern. Capricorn, Southern. Is that going to be on the test tomorrow?"

"Yeah," answered Peter. "Geography's my best subject, but I still think it would be easier to remember if we could actually see what we were studying."

"Me too," agreed Henrik. "It'd be great to actually go there."

"Yeah. I'd just like to see where the big line is—you know, for the equator."

Henrik laughed. "You'll do fine. You always do better than I do. I have to study twice as hard as you and Elise."

"Not anymore. All of a sudden, you're becoming smarter. And you say you actually went to the library?"

"Of course I went to the library," replied Henrik, defensively. "Like any good scholar. And I even checked out this book, see?" He pointed at it with his nose and started counting again under his breath.

"*Sailing Illustrated*. Looks pretty good." Peter leaned over, picked up the book, and thumbed through the diagrams of sails and photos of different kinds of sailboats. There were even pages on how to tie knots. He glanced at the front flap, where students wrote their names and classrooms in front of the due-date stamp.

"Hey, did you see who checked this book out before you?" Peter placed the open book in front of his friend.

Henrik stopped his push-ups, looked inside the cover, and smiled.

"So that's how Elise knows so much about sailing. Well, maybe we can learn a little something, too!"

SETTING SAIL

Henrik led the charge down the school stairs Friday afternoon. Peter was close on his heels.

"Finally!" shouted Henrik, jumping down to the first-floor landing. He clicked his heels and did a little jig.

"Walk, please, Mr. Melchior," came the bass drum voice of their principal. He was around the corner, but everyone knew Mr. Jensen could see around corners. He had periscope vision.

"Yes, sir, Mr. Jensen," replied Henrik, catching himself and slowing down. It was no good trying to run inside the school building while Mr. Jensen was around. Peter put on the brakes behind Henrik and canceled what he was about to yell. As they tiptoed by the office where Mr. Jensen was stationed outside the door, Peter felt like a rocket roped down on the launching pad.

"Have a good vacation, boys," boomed the principal. He rocked up on his heels when he spoke, a slight smile on his lips, his hands behind his back.

"Yes, sir," replied Peter. "We will."

Neither boy said anything more until they stepped outside the three-story brick building. Then Henrik cut loose with a wild whoop.

"Here we go!" he hollered.

"Yeah!"

The boys raced neck and neck all the way to the harbor, but Elise was already waiting for them outside Grandfather's boathouse.

"How did you get here so soon?" asked Peter, catching his breath.

Elise grinned. "My class let out five minutes early. How did you do on your last test?"

Henrik looked over at Peter. "How did we do, Peter?"

Peter grinned. "We passed. What else?"

"Oh, I don't know," replied Elise. "I just thought maybe you boys might have been held back a grade—you know, because you like school so much."

"Come on, Elise." Peter gave his sister a playful nudge. "Are you ready to try the mast?"

With the boat sitting right side up next to the boathouse, the boys held the new mast in place while Elise tightened the three ropes holding it up—one to each side and one stretching down to the front end of the boat. Then came their biggest test.

"Ready for the sail?" asked Peter, running into the boathouse to find it. Elise had made loops of rope to hold the sail to the mast, and the boys tied them on securely while Elise slowly pulled up the sail with a long clothesline.

"Hey, not bad," said Elise, admiring their work. "Should we see if it really sails?"

"One day early?" questioned Peter.

"Why not?" answered Henrik, picking up the back end of the boat.

Careful not to bump anything, they carried it down to the pier, then gently slid it down to the dock where the *Anna Marie* was usually tied up.

"I can't believe your uncle is still on his honeymoon," said

Henrik, looking at the empty boat slip.

Elise frowned. "What's wrong with that?"

"Nothing." Henrik set his side of the boat down on the edge of the dock. "Just seems like a long time to be gone. Where did they go, anyway?"

"Somewhere in Sweden," answered Elise, pausing to look out to sea. "Grandfather knows, but he's not telling anyone."

"Watch it! We don't want to scrape the bottom," warned Peter as he let his side drop gently into the still water. The trim little rowboat turned sailboat floated happily next to the dock, and Elise tied it securely.

"So"—Henrik looked from Peter to Elise—"should we see if it works?"

Elise hesitated. "I don't know."

"We'll need three life jackets," said Peter, turning back up to run to the boathouse. "Plus the oars."

"And don't forget a bucket to bail water if it leaks," added Henrik.

"It's getting foggy out there," worried Elise. She fiddled with the rope that would pull in the sail as it swung from one side of the boat to the other. The main sheet, she called it. Peter couldn't figure out why it was called a sheet and not a rope.

A minute later, Henrik and Peter returned with their arms full of orange cork life jackets, a bucket, and a pair of oars.

"Should we tell anyone where we're going?" asked Elise.

Peter tossed the life jackets into the boat. "We looked for Grandfather, but he wasn't at the boathouse yet. I wrote him a note to tell him we're going out for a test sail."

"We won't be gone long," Henrik added. "Just a few minutes."

Henrik took his place at the tiller—the stick attached to the rudder—while Elise hopped in and pulled in the sail. Before Peter could untie the ropes holding their little boat in place, the sail filled, and their boat pulled ahead like a horse ready to run.

"Hold it a minute!" yelled Peter, scrambling from one rope to the next. "Don't leave me here." Peter finally undid the second rope, pushed off from the dock, and dove for the boat. "Here we go!"

A puff of wind caught them and sent the little boat surging ahead.

Henrik was beaming from ear to ear, gripping the tiller as if he wasn't quite sure what to do with it.

In the middle of the boat, Peter tried to find a balance that would keep the boat even. He looked back at Henrik as they zig-zagged wildly around a couple of work boats tied up next to their pier.

"Are you sure you know what you're doing?" Peter asked him.

"We know what we're doing—don't we, Elise?" Henrik asked back.

For a moment, Peter thought his sister looked worried, but then she flashed a smile.

"Sure. You guys read the book, too."

"Yes, ma'am!" said Henrik, pushing the tiller back and forth. He whooped as the wind picked up their little boat. They nearly flew through the harbor. Behind them, they left a boiling trail of white foam.

Peter dug his fingernails into the side railing of the boat as they tipped lower toward the water. "Maybe we should have picked a calmer day."

"No way!" exclaimed Henrik, correcting their course around the back end of a ferry from Sweden. "This is great, don't you think?"

The ferry's horn blasted, and Peter jumped. But he had to admit that sailing was fun, once you got the feel for it. "It's just so different from being in Uncle Morten's big boat. Do you remember the last time we were in this boat together?"

"It wasn't like this, though," Elise said. "Escaping to Sweden was different."

"Yeah," agreed Henrik. "A lot different."

No one said anything for a minute. A seagull swooped low to

race them, and Peter's eyes followed it until it disappeared. "So where are we going?"

"Anywhere!" Henrik smiled and scooped up a handful of water to splash Peter. "Maybe China!"

Peter ducked but got wet anyway. Suddenly, he noticed they were getting awfully close to a large ship. "Better watch where we're going, Henrik," he warned. "Remember the mines."

"Would you quit worrying? There aren't any mines."

Peter wasn't so sure, and Elise pulled the sail in tighter as the side of the ship grew taller.

"We're getting awfully close, Henrik," Peter worried as he looked around his sister at the ship.

"No problem, Peter. I see it."

Elise looked back, too. "Peter's right, Henrik. We're going to have to tack."

"Tack," repeated Henrik. "How do we do that again?"

"Push the stick toward the sail," instructed Elise. "I'll take care of the rest."

Peter leaned out for a better view. "We're going to hit that boat in two seconds, Henrik."

"Okay, here we go!" said Henrik. But instead of pushing his steering stick toward the sail as Elise had told him, he jerked it away.

"Toward the sail!" yelled Elise. "*Toward* the sail!"

But it was too late. Henrik steered them away from the ship they were about to hit, but in the wrong direction. The sail came snapping across with the full force of the wind, and the boom—the pole along the bottom of the sail—knocked Peter in the head just above his right ear.

"Are you all right?" asked Henrik, horrified.

Peter bent over and groaned.

"Peter, are you okay?" Elise asked him. "That really hit you."

"I'll say." Peter didn't want to open his eyes, it hurt so badly. But he sat back up and looked around, still holding his head.

"Next time you do that, I better duck." Peter looked back at

Henrik, who was white in the face.

"I'm awfully sorry, Peter. I didn't mean to hit you."

"I know. And I'm okay, really." But his head still throbbed as their little boat shot out through the opening in the harbor breakwater and into the open water. Elise ducked as a cloud of icy-fine salt spray peppered them in the face. Peter had to smile; it was his favorite smell.

Henrik steered their little boat close to the shore, following a rocky beach around the castle. But once they had passed the last tower, he looked out at the sound toward Sweden.

"Look out there," he told them, pointing.

A bank of fog was moving in swiftly, ahead of a wind that had suddenly changed direction. It almost looked like an advancing army, solid and gray against the blue of the water and the sky.

Elise stared out at the advancing fog. "I think we better head back in."

"Yeah," agreed Peter. "If we stay out past dinnertime, we'll catch it."

Henrik looked disappointed but nodded his head. "I don't think Christopher Columbus would have turned around so quickly."

"And I'll bet he didn't have a mom to worry about him, either," added Peter.

"Okay, okay, I'm turning."

This time, Henrik turned the boat just as Elise told him to— nice and easy, pushing the steering tiller in the right direction. The sail flapped briefly as they came into the wind, then filled as they headed back in the direction they had come. And the little Danish flag Elise had sewn fluttered eagerly in the fresh breeze.

But already the billowing cloud was overtaking them, and soon they found themselves surrounded by soft, moist, gray fog.

"Wow, this is weird," commented Henrik.

Peter stuck out his tongue to taste the low-flying cloud. "Kind of like someone threw a big, wet blanket over our heads."

The wind settled down to a whisper, barely filling the sail.

"Who turned off the motor?" asked Peter.

Henrik pushed the tiller back and forth, trying to make the boat wiggle along. When the harbor foghorn started blasting, Peter nearly jumped out of his seat.

"Which direction did that come from?" asked Elise.

"That way." Henrik pointed forward.

"No, that way." Peter pointed in the opposite direction.

"Well, we're not going to make it home at this speed," decided Elise. "I'm going to take this sail down."

As Elise let loose the rope holding it up, Peter caught the dead sail and wrestled it to the side and out of the way. "I'll row first," he volunteered. Since no one argued, he took the oars from the bottom of the boat and locked them into place. The foghorn blasted again, and he started pulling in the direction he thought the sound came from.

"I don't think we're going the right way," said Elise after about five minutes. She pointed off to the side. "It sounds like the foghorn is over there."

Peter paused, listened again to the blast, and shook his head. "I don't think so, Elise."

"Well, right now we're just going around in circles," Henrik observed.

Peter frowned and listened once more. Maybe they were right. The foghorn didn't sound quite as loud now, and it did seem to come from behind them. *I'm not sure where it's coming from,* he thought.

"Well," Peter finally admitted. "Maybe you're right."

"It's tricky in this fog," said Elise from her lookout position in the front of the boat. "I can hardly tell where the sound is coming from, either, Peter. But I do think we need to turn around."

Then Peter heard something else in the fog—a laugh, and then men's voices, far off.

"Shh," whispered Henrik. "Did you hear that?"

Peter nodded. "Sounds like people. We must be close to the harbor."

They spent the next ten minutes quickly rowing toward the voices, then stopping to listen, then rowing again. But still they seemed to be going in circles, never closer to the voices, never closer to the foghorn. And the fog was thicker than ever.

"Wow, I can barely see you, Elise," said Henrik, laughing. "This fog is really something. Even the water seems strange."

He reached down into the sea and made a terrible face.

"Oh, yuk!" he said, shaking his hand.

Peter paused at the oars to look closer.

"Look," Henrik told them, holding up his hand. It was covered in black splotches that ran down his arm. "Oil."

"Wait a minute," chimed in Elise. "Maybe this is the same spot where we picked up the strange guy with the skunk beard."

Peter looked over the side. "Think his boat is down there?"

Elise swung around and grabbed Peter's hands. "Peter, stop the boat!" she whispered urgently.

At that moment, Peter heard men's voices once more—the same voices they had been hearing in the fog for the past half hour. And this time there was no mistaking them. The voices were close enough that they could have come from inside the little rowboat.

Peter glanced over his shoulder and immediately saw why Elise was so concerned. In the fog, they had nearly rowed straight toward the front end of a large boat. It was larger than their uncle's boat and painted a grimy black. The front sides were bare of the numbers that would identify it as a Danish fishing boat. More like a ugly work boat, it had a square wheelhouse up front.

Out of sight toward the back of the boat, someone coughed. Peter quickly rowed backward to slip deeper into the safety of the fog.

"I've heard enough of your complaining," scolded one of the men. His voice was scratchy, loud and German.

"He's speaking German," whispered Henrik, leaning forward in his seat. "What's he saying?"

"Shh!" Peter whispered back.

"Complaining?" came another voice. Peter shivered at the sound. All of the German soldiers had left Helsingor by now. *There can't be any more Germans around,* he told himself. *Can there?* He strained to understand what the men were talking about.

"What are they saying, Elise?" Peter whispered the question to the one person in their boat who could understood the most German. But she reacted the same way he had.

"Shh," she told him.

Peter could make out a word or two here and there. Something about "let's go now" and "Rio."

"Did he say something about Rio?" Peter asked his sister once more. "Like the city in South America?"

Elise nodded her head and held her finger to her lips. "The other man is mad because their boat sank," she finally whispered back. "Now they have to fish something up out of it before they can leave. I think that's what they're arguing about."

She listened some more, tilting her head to catch everything. "A schedule," she whispered to Peter. "Staying on a schedule, meeting someone. One man is asking the other why they can't just leave now. They ... uh ... already have enough ... something about coins, about gold."

"Gold?" Peter whispered, louder this time. "What do you mean, gold?"

Elise just shook her head. "I don't know. I didn't catch that part."

Without realizing it, Peter had allowed their little boat to drift closer to the larger fishing vessel. The men stopped talking, then a cranking sound began.

"Ready?" someone shouted above the din of the clanking.

"Ready!" said someone else. A swell pushed them even closer as Henrik tapped on Peter's hand. He pointed away from the boat with his thumb.

"Let's get out of here," Henrik whispered into Peter's face. "We're too close."

And they were. Peter looked over his shoulder, and the fog seemed to lighten at just the wrong moment. A second later, Peter was staring at two men standing above them on the deck of the black boat. One was tall and wide-shouldered, a powerful-looking man in a white T-shirt. The other, lean and wiry, was dressed in green coveralls, the kind auto mechanics wore. They both stood on the deck with their backs to the rowboat, busily attaching a deep-sea diving helmet onto a third man. There was a small crane above them, and a full collection of pumps, generators, and hoses.

Now Peter was sure. This was the same boat they had seen from their lookout at Kronborg Castle the Sunday before!

6

A RISKY EXPEDITION

"Let's go," Elise hissed into his ear.

Peter didn't need any prodding—he was eager to get away from the boat as fast as possible. But as he rowed, one of the oars made a terrible squeak. And one of the German men glanced over his shoulder.

"Row, Peter!" yelled Henrik. "It's the guy with the skunk beard!"

Peter felt panicky—the same kind of heart-pounding fear he had felt nearly two years earlier when they were escaping from the Germans in the very same little boat. Peter had been rowing then, too. And now it was happening all over again. He shook the memory from his throbbing head, dug in his oars, and pulled with all his strength.

"Which way?" he grunted.

"Just get us out of here," replied Elise. That was all the direction Peter needed.

They shot back into the fog, rowing as fast as Peter's arms would take them. In between his gasps for air, Peter waited for the sound of the big fishing boat's engine. But there was nothing.

He listened for the Helsingor foghorn. For some reason, it had stopped sounding. Either they were too far away to hear it, or it was no longer foggy at the harbor.

"It's getting lighter," announced Elise from the front. The sun glowed through the fog around them. Still Peter rowed, listening, and still there was no sound other than the waves and the swish and squeak of his rowing. If they had been traveling in the right direction, they should be nearing the harbor. At least the Germans hadn't started up their boat and chased them.

Elise twisted around and looked back into the fog. "Do you hear anything?" she asked.

Peter shook his head and looked back over his own shoulder. He slowed his rowing, then counted fifty strokes. They were almost out into the full sunshine again, and heading in the right direction.

"Helsingor, straight ahead," announced Elise.

"Wow," breathed Henrik. "What was all that about back there?"

Elise had begun to fill him in on the Germans' conversation when they were interrupted by the throb of a powerful engine coming at them out of the fog. Peter saw a stubby front end emerge from the mist, then a tall wheelhouse.

"It's the *Vulkan*," he said, stopping his rowing long enough to wave with one hand. "Hey, Captain Bering!"

A minute later, their friend slowed his boat down long enough to come alongside. Peter, Elise, and Henrik held on as the waves from the tug rocked them. "What are you kids doing out here in this fog?" the captain yelled down at them. "I could have run you over."

Henrik grinned back up at Captain Bering. "We were just trying out our new sailboat when we got caught in the fog. And—"

"Guess what? We just ran into old Skunk Beard out there!" Peter pointed at the way they had come through the fog. "The man we rescued from the sinking boat. He's out there with some kind of diving rig."

Captain Bering seemed to understand exactly what Peter was saying.

"How long ago?" he asked.

"About fifteen minutes," replied Elise.

The tugboat skipper backed his boat away from them. "Thanks for the information. You kids should head home right away."

Captain Bering ducked back into the wheelhouse, spun the *Vulkan* around in a whirlpool of foam, and headed cautiously away. Peter, Elise, and Henrik stared after the boat until it faded into the fog.

"I hope Captain Bering can find them," Henrik finally said as they passed the breakwater and found their way past the ships in the harbor. Now that the afternoon fog had lifted, it was almost as if nothing had happened out on the water.

Elise looked back out in the direction from which they had come. "It's still pretty foggy out there."

They quickly tied up the oil-stained little boat and ran back up to the boathouse.

"We'll clean the boat up after dinner," said Peter. "It's already almost six. If we're not home in about two minutes, we'll be in trouble."

As they ran past the boathouse, Peter stopped for a moment to check on his grandfather.

"Grandfather, are you in there?" Peter yelled as he pushed open the door. But there was no sign of anyone—only the flutter of the homing pigeons they kept in one half of the shed. The note he had written for his grandfather was just where he had left it, propped against a can of paint in the middle of the workbench.

"Wonder where he went?" Peter murmured to himself as he hurried to catch up with Henrik and Elise, who were already down the street. Peter turned to take one last look at the harbor. He nearly fell over at what he saw.

The Germans' black boat was just slipping in through the breakwater. Peter stopped and stared, unable to take his eyes off the boat as it moved into a space behind an old fireboat. Heart pounding, he chased after the others.

"Wait up!" Peter shouted. "Hey, wait for me!"

Half a block down the street, Henrik stopped by a corner lamppost.

"Come on, Peter," said Elise. "We're going to be late. What took you so long back there?"

"I was just checking to see if Grandfather was at the boathouse"—Peter couldn't get the words out fast enough—"and I saw the black boat coming in!"

Henrik straightened up, his eyes wide. "No kidding?"

Peter nodded. "They found a spot between two boats over near the gas docks."

Elise looked in the direction of the harbor, although they couldn't see the water anymore because of all the buildings. "They must have slipped past Captain Bering," she said nervously. "We need to tell Mom and Dad about what's going on— about the Germans and everything."

Peter and Henrik agreed.

"Yeah, and just think—if they really do have Nazi treasure, we'll be heroes for stopping them!" noted Henrik.

The big bells of Helsingor Cathedral boomed six times as Peter led the way back home to their street. He was the first one up the stairs and through their front door. But their apartment was as quiet and empty as the boathouse.

"Mom?" called Peter, looking into the dark kitchen. Nothing was even cooking on the stove.

"Dad? We're home!" Elise hurried down the hallway, but the bedrooms were empty.

Henrik looked puzzled. "Where is everyone?"

"Here, look at this," said Elise, picking up a note off the kitchen table. Peter wondered why he hadn't noticed it when he walked in. "It's from Mom. It says, 'Your father had a retirement dinner for someone at the bank, and I'm going along. You can warm up some ham and potatoes. We should be home by eight-thirty at the latest. Call your grandfather if you need anything. Love, Mom.' "

"But we had ham and potatoes last night," complained Peter, searching the kitchen cupboards for something else.

"That gives us just enough time!" exclaimed Henrik.

"To eat?" Peter wasn't sure what Henrik was talking about.

" 'Course not." Henrik headed back toward the door. "If we hurry, maybe we can see what the Germans on that boat are really up to. We can't let them get away!"

"Oh no," groaned Elise. "What do we need to do that for?"

"All we're going to do is peek," explained Henrik. "I'll bet they didn't see us up close when we were out on the water, so they wouldn't recognize us even if they do see us. Let's just go see what that diving expedition is all about. You know, gather evidence."

Peter shook his head. "I think Elise is right, Henrik. We should wait here until my parents get back, and then tell them what's going on. I don't want to get near those Germans. Besides, I'm hungry."

Henrik picked up a loaf of bread from the counter and took Peter by the arm. "I don't, either. But we'll have more to tell your parents if we're sure about what we saw. And besides, you don't want me to go alone, do you?"

"We should at least leave a note," declared Elise, looking for a pencil.

"No time," replied Henrik, pulling Peter toward the door. "And we'll be back before your folks get home."

"Why does it always end up like this?" Peter asked his sister as they hurried back down the stairs. He frowned as he chewed on a piece of dark rye bread.

The gas dock was where all the small boats in the harbor tied up to get fuel—a busy place of comings and goings. But at six-thirty on a still-light Friday evening, it looked deserted. As they walked closer, Peter spotted two older work boats tied up side by side near the end of the dock.

"Is this where you saw it?" whispered Henrik.

"I thought so," answered Peter, hoping it was gone. "But now I'm not so sure."

"Maybe they left again," said Elise, sounding as hopeful as Peter.

But they kept walking quietly to the end of the pier, glancing between rusting ships and old fishing boats. The end of the pier was rarely used, and Peter could see the dark water of the harbor between several rotting boards. This wasn't somewhere they visited very often.

At the end of the pier rested an ancient fireboat, half torn apart for scrap metal. Behind it, almost hidden from view, Peter barely made out the top of another boat.

"There it is," said Henrik. He motioned with his eyes but didn't point. "Come on."

Peter and Elise crept along beside Henrik as he climbed up and over the wrecked fireboat. All the windows were gone, and someone had begun to remove the sides of the cabin. Peter looked around nervously, then down at the black boat. It was much larger than it had seemed out in the fog—at least the same size as Captain Bering's tugboat.

"Do you think anyone's on board?" whispered Peter.

"I don't know," decided Henrik, hopping down from their hiding place. "But I'm going to find out."

"What are you, crazy?" Peter whispered loudly after him.

"Henrik!" warned Elise.

Henrik only paused for a second.

"Look," said Elise. "If anyone comes, I'll whistle."

Henrik nodded and took a deep breath. Then he hopped down onto the hidden boat as if he were going for a friendly visit and strolled right up to a side doorway. Peter couldn't make himself follow.

"Hello, there," called Henrik as Peter and Elise looked nervously up and around. There still was no one else on the pier. "Anyone home?"

Henrik knocked sharply on the door, then waited. There was no sign that anyone was inside. He jiggled the door handle. Locked. Henrik looked back at the twins and smiled.

"See?" he shouted, waving for them to follow. "I knew there was no one here."

Peter's heart was pumping double time by then, but still he stood up. One part of him wanted to run straight home. *But what exactly is under all those tarps?*

"I'm going to see what's on board," he told his sister.

Elise glanced at the pier behind them and bit her lip. "I'll keep watch."

"Look at this!" Henrik exclaimed as soon as Peter joined him. He pulled back one of the tarps. "This looks like the diving suit. And here—what about this?"

Peter picked up a crate the size of a small chest. Henrik pulled off the top.

"Empty," said Henrik, but a tiny glimmer caught Peter's eye.

"Wait a minute, Henrik. What's that?"

They looked more closely at the bottom of the crate. In a corner crack where the sides met the bottom, Peter could barely make out something shiny.

"Here, let me see that," said Henrik. He turned the crate upside down and tapped it on the boat's deck. When something fell out, both boys just stared.

"Is that what I think it is?" asked Peter. They both bent down, bumping their heads together.

"Ow!" said Henrik, picking up the shiny gold object and holding it up for them both to see.

Peter rubbed his head for the second time that day, then tried to read the inscription on what looked like an ancient gold coin.

"I knew it!" cried Henrik excitedly. "Skunk Beard has the Nazi treasure! And now we can prove it."

"I don't believe it," said Peter, staring at the gleaming coin. "But that would explain why he was so worried about his boat."

"Right!" Henrik said triumphantly. "I knew something like

this would happen. This is what I've been trying to tell you and Elise. I'll bet the rest of the treasure is somewhere on this boat."

"Let me see the coin for a minute," insisted Peter.

Henrik stood still enough for Peter to study the coin. A lion, or a leopard wearing a crown, was etched into one side; on the other was a shield design. The border was ringed with strange writing. "Looks like Latin." Peter whistled. "This is old, Henrik. Really old. Now we really better go tell my parents about this."

Henrik held on to the coin and walked over to the locked door again. "I just wish we could get in."

"No way," said Peter. "We've seen enough. Here, let's put this tarp back the way we found—"

Peter was interrupted by a low whistle from where Elise was keeping watch. Peter and Henrik stared at each other in horror.

"Where do we go?" whispered Henrik.

But Peter didn't have a chance to answer before Elise came tumbling down to the deck from her hiding place.

"Hide!" she ordered. "There are three of them, and they're running down the pier. Skunk Beard, too!"

Henrik and the twins didn't even have time to climb back up to the other boat. In a moment of panic, they twirled around, looking for a place, any place, to hide. Now that they were sure who these men were, Peter had no intention of meeting them face-to-face.

"Here," Elise finally whispered. Peter could hear the men's steps coming closer, climbing over the boat next to them.

Elise lifted the canvas cover to a small lifeboat on the rear deck of the black trawler, and they piled in just as the men jumped down to the deck of their boat.

"Hurry," said one of the men.

Henrik had his elbow in Peter's side, but Peter buried his face in his knees and tried to stay perfectly still under the heavy canvas cover.

"What are we doing in here?" he whispered to his sister. "Let's just run for it!"

"No!" Henrik objected. "Wait until they start their motor, then jump out on the count of three."

I don't care if they do see us, thought Peter, starting to panic. *Let's just get out of here.*

The men were yelling and grunting at one another, and it sounded as if they were pushing things around on deck.

"What's he saying?" Henrik asked Elise.

"One of them is ordering the other around," replied Elise in her quietest whisper. Peter could feel her shivering—or maybe it was him. "He just told him to tie it all down so it doesn't blow away once they're out on the water."

"Tie what down?" asked Henrik, but Elise didn't answer. The footsteps of one of the men were coming closer. He was grumbling something Peter couldn't quite make out.

The footsteps stopped right next to the small lifeboat, and there was another grunt. Peter could feel the canvas being stretched and moved around his back. Then something like a rope slapped against him once, then again.

Peter's back itched. *What's he doing out there?*

Suddenly, Peter had a sinking feeling. The little crack between the top edge of the boat and the canvas had been covered. Now, Peter couldn't see his hand in front of his face.

Then just as suddenly as the footsteps had approached, they were gone again. More yelling, and then the roar of an engine starting up rumbled from almost directly beneath them.

"What was he doing?" asked Henrik. "I thought he was going to find us."

"He was doing something with the tarp," said Elise over the roar of the engine. "The other German was yelling at him to make sure nothing was loose."

"I don't care what they do," Peter finally said, trying to sit up. "I'm getting out of here."

But he couldn't even straighten up—the canvas top of their lifeboat had been securely tied down. For a moment, Peter felt a surge of panic.

"I can't budge this tarp," he said, raising his voice. No one except Henrik and Elise could hear him over the roar of the engine.

"Here, help me get this loose so we can get out of here."

Elise and Henrik joined in the struggle as they all three pushed up against the heavy canvas. By that time, Peter had given up all thought of trying to hide what they were doing.

"They're going to spot us for sure," said Henrik.

"Doesn't matter anymore," answered Elise.

"We have to get out of here," added Peter. He pushed with all his strength against the canvas cover, but all he could do was stretch it slightly.

"Isn't there a crack somewhere around the edge we could slip through?" asked Peter. The engine underneath them roared even louder, and they felt the boat sway.

Even though the air wasn't hot, Peter was sweating and breathing hard. For a second, he felt as if he was going to faint. Still, he kept feeling all the way around, trying to find a gap in the canvas large enough to slip his hands through.

"We should have jumped out when we had the chance," Peter fumed. He wanted to kick himself, but instead pounded the side of the boat and gave out a yell.

"Hey!" he shouted. "Hey!"

Henrik grabbed his arm. "What are you doing, Peter? They'll hear us!"

"I hope so. Maybe then we can still get off of this boat—jump into the water. But we *have* to get off this boat before they leave the harbor!"

Henrik and Elise were quiet for only a moment, then Elise spoke up.

"He's right, Henrik." She raised her voice with Peter's. "HEY! LET US OUT!"

Finally, Henrik joined their yelling, screaming, and pounding. But they couldn't get past the canvas cover, and they couldn't seem to make any noise that would make the Germans hear them.

"I can't believe it," Peter said after a while, his voice hoarse. Underneath them, the boat rocked and swayed. He figured they were well out of the harbor. "No one can hear us."

"It's that old engine," yelled Henrik. "It's too loud."

"Well, if they walk past us, they'll hear us," added Elise hopefully. "And they'd see us pushing at the cover if they would only look."

"Yeah, but they must not be anywhere near us," concluded Henrik. "We're here on the back end of the boat, behind all the cargo and diving stuff."

Peter curled up in a ball in the bottom of the lifeboat and tried to get comfortable. *There must be a way out of this*, he told himself.

"It's all my fault," said Henrik, his voice cracking. "It's all my fault."

"Well, that doesn't matter now," snapped Elise. "We just have to figure out a way to get ourselves out of this mess. I wish one of us had a pocketknife."

Peter thought of his little red pocketknife resting on top of the dresser at home. He promised himself he would never take it out of his pocket again.

"Which way do you think we're going?" Henrik wondered aloud. "North or south?"

"I guarantee you these Germans aren't going back to Germany," said Elise. "We're headed toward the open ocean."

"But this old tugboat can't go too far, can it?" Peter hit the side of the boat with his fist.

"I don't know," Elise answered. "Remember, we made it all the way to Sweden in a rowboat."

All of them sat still for a while, surrounded by the roar of the powerful engine. It was so much louder than the friendly *chug-cough* of their Uncle Morten's old fishing boat. But then, this wasn't exactly an old fishing boat. After a while, Peter held his ears.

He tried to feel the ocean swells, tried to guess where they were. His stomach rumbled. A feeling of panic grew inside him.

"Elise!" he told his sister. "Dad and Mom are going to go crazy. They'll probably send the police out after us."

"You thought of that, too? They're going to go down to the harbor, see that the sailboat is in the water, all covered with oil. Then they're really going to wonder. I should have left a note like I was going to."

"What about that other note we left?" wondered Henrik.

Peter scratched his head. "It was still in the boathouse when I checked. Grandfather hadn't been there since we left it."

"Yeah, but they'll find it, won't they?" Henrik sounded hopeful.

"Even if they do, it won't do any good." Peter scowled in the darkness. "It won't help them find us way out here."

He couldn't hear her, but Peter thought he could feel Elise crying.

7

PRISONERS ON THE OPEN SEA

Peter wasn't sure what woke him. Their prison was still dark, and the engine still rumbled below them. But something felt different. He shook the groggy feeling from his head and looked around. The black trawler seemed to be powering over long ocean swells. The waves didn't feel at all like the choppy waves they were used to in the sound—the kind of waves that pounded into a boat and tossed spray all around. He cleared his throat, and it tasted like the exhaust fumes from the boat engine.

"Elise? Henrik? Are you guys awake?"

"I'm awake, Peter," answered Elise. "You boys have been asleep for hours."

"How long?"

"All night, I'd guess. We're somewhere out on the ocean now." Elise's voice sounded flat and drained of emotion. But she touched his hand.

"Look, I think I've got a plan for how we can break out of here," she told Peter. "I've just been waiting for you to wake up."

"Yeah?"

"I wish I'd thought of this before. I haven't been able to make it work on my own." In the dark, she touched his hand with something metal.

"What's that?" Peter jumped from his curled up position and bumped his sore head on the heavy canvas.

"My belt buckle. If we bend it apart, we can make something sharp out of it. I've been working at it, but I can't do it. You try."

Peter took the belt and felt the buckle. The thin metal was looped around into the narrow leather belt. If he could bend it apart like a wire coat hanger, he would have a sharp edge. And then what?

"So what do we do with it if we do get it apart?" Peter asked. They were getting used to shouting above the constant roar of the engine. He shifted to stretch his legs and bumped into Henrik.

"Huh?" mumbled Henrik. "Hey, what's going on?"

Peter could tell Henrik was just as confused as Peter had been when he woke up.

"Elise and I are right here." Peter reached out and felt Henrik's knee.

"Oh, okay." Henrik cleared his throat. "I must have dropped off for a minute."

"Elise says we've been asleep for hours," Peter told him. "I was hoping this was a bad dream."

"Me too."

"But, Henrik," Peter said. "Elise has an escape plan. If we can pry apart her belt buckle, we'll have something sharp, and—"

"Let me see it," interrupted Henrik. Peter handed it to him; a moment later there was a grunt and a snap.

"Got it," Henrik announced triumphantly. "It's like a broken wire."

"I was thinking we could use it to poke through the canvas," Elise told them.

"Maybe," Henrik said a little doubtfully. "It's better than just sitting here."

The three of them took turns scratching at the canvas, working away slowly in one long line at the fabric. When Peter's arm got tired, he passed the buckle to Elise. After a few minutes, she gave it to Henrik.

"It's not doing a thing," Henrik finally said in disgust. "First these Germans are knot maniacs, tying down the cover. Then they have to use indestructible canvas. I thought they lost the war."

"My turn," said Peter. He scratched a little more at the canvas, trying to wear away a hole.

"Hey, look," he observed after a few minutes. "I think it's actually working."

Henrik leaned in for a look. "Let me see."

"I don't see anything," said Elise.

"Peter's right," exclaimed Henrik. "There's a hole!"

Without warning, the roar of the boat engines slowed, and their world started rocking even more.

"We're stopping somewhere," said Elise. "Quick! Let me take a turn."

Instead, Peter attacked the canvas even more fiercely, working at it faster and faster. He ignored his sister's hand on his arm.

"I've got it," he insisted. "Let me finish."

By that time, the boat had stopped, and the engine slowed down to a murmuring idle. Big waves tossed them around, and they could hear the yelling of men over the engine.

"Hear that?" asked Henrik.

"People yelling," replied Elise.

"Yeah, but there are more voices than before." Henrik put his ear up close to the canvas. "I think we're docking somewhere. Elise, can you tell what they're saying?"

If we've made it to a harbor, Peter wondered, *then why are we still rocking around as if we're out in the middle of the ocean?* He didn't say anything, though; he just kept scraping at the tarp until he felt like he was going to faint.

"What do you hear, Elise?" Henrik finally asked.

"I hear new voices, like you said."

"See?" Henrik sounded relieved. "They'll just shut down the engine now, and we can get out of here."

"But the other voices are German, too."

"Do you think we're in Germany?" asked Henrik. "I guess that's okay. The war's over. We'll be able to get home fine."

With one last vicious push, Peter tore through the canvas with a satisfying rip. He smiled to himself as Henrik and Elise helped him pull the tear until at last the hole was big enough for one of them to poke his head through.

"Here, let me," started Henrik.

"No, let Peter," Elise said. "He's the one who made the hole."

Peter looked at his sister and Henrik in the dim pink light coming through the hole. The boat was still rocking, though not as much, and the engine idled calmly. The fresh, cold salt smell of the sea entered through the hole.

"Okay," agreed Peter. He listened once more, heard nothing new, then carefully pushed his head through the rip. What he saw made him catch his breath.

Henrik was tugging at his arm. Peter swatted him away and pulled his head back quickly.

"What's out there?" whispered Elise.

"We're out at sea," replied Peter, ducking lower. "No land in sight."

"So why did we stop?" Henrik moved toward the light. "I'm going to take a look."

Peter grabbed his friend by the shoulders and pulled hard.

"What are you doing?" asked Henrik, rolling backward. "What's the big idea?"

"You can't stick your head out there!" Peter warned him. "We're sitting right next to a huge German submarine, and they're loading all kinds of boxes from this boat into it."

"How do we know it's not a British submarine?" Henrik ventured after a moment. "Or maybe American?"

They heard a man shout over the sound of the engine.

"*Vorsicht!*" roared the gruff voice.

"Does that answer your question?" asked Peter. "Henrik, even you know that much German."

"Vorsicht," repeated Henrik. "Be careful."

"And if the German words don't answer your question, the sub's ugly red-and-black flag will."

Elise groaned and leaned against her brother. "This can't be happening, Peter."

Peter strained to figure out what was happening. As best he could tell, they were a night's voyage out into the ocean—probably somewhere south of Norway in the North Sea. And now these Germans were unloading supplies and other boxes into a submarine—a submarine that was still flying the Nazi flag a month and a half after the Germans had surrendered.

It was all like a bad dream, and there seemed to be no way out. Even if they did escape their hiding place, what would the men do to them?

"Peter, what do you think we should do?" Elise asked her brother.

Peter slapped his forehead with his palm, trying to think. *God, what do you think we should do?* he prayed. *Wait here? Risk it?* He looked up through the slit in the canvas at the pink clouds, hoping for an answer. The boat was grinding up hard against the side of the German submarine, but no one outside seemed to care.

"Let's wait and see what happens," Peter finally said. "Maybe they'll finish unloading their boxes, and we can head back to land."

The idea seemed to make sense, so they all sat still. Then the engine shut down completely, and they heard a new sound—the sturdy, powerful hum of the submarine's diesel engines.

"How big is that thing?" Henrik asked quietly. "I'd like to take a peek."

"No, Henrik," Peter warned him. "Really. Someone might see us."

Henrik frowned but made no move to look out.

"It's huge, Henrik. Even bigger than I imagined." In his mind, Peter pictured the low, gleaming gray deck, like the top of a giant whale. He had seen it for only a moment when he poked his head up into the early morning light. But it looked much larger in real life than in the pictures he had seen in the newspapers. Tip to tip, it was better than twice as long as the boat they were on. *Nearly as long as a soccer field*, Peter guessed. A big cannon-type gun was mounted just behind the tall central tower, and the tower itself stood about fifteen feet above deck. There were no numbers on the side, but instead someone had painted a lucky horseshoe near the top. Above that, the main tower was crowned by a collection of periscope poles and antennae.

Peter knew that this was what the Germans called a U-boat— the U standing for undersea.

"Come on!" shouted a voice from outside, and their boat again took a sharp blow against the massive submarine.

"This is really weird," commented Henrik. "I know this is an old boat, but we're going to have a hole in the side if they don't watch out."

There was more shouting, scrambling around on the deck, and the submarine's engines roared with power.

"Good!" said Elise. "They're leaving."

"Maybe now we can get—" began Peter. He was interrupted by a loud explosion that shook their hiding place and rocked the boat they were on.

"What?" Peter began as splinters of wood rained down on them. A moment later, they could feel their world tipping as the front of the big boat began to dip into the ocean.

"We've got to get out of here," Peter decided without hesitating. Germans or no Germans, he had no intention of going down with the ship.

As the boat rocked and swayed at an alarming angle, he and Henrik pulled and kicked at the cover so they could all escape.

Peter's first sight was the trawler's half-destroyed forward cabin. The front end had been blown off, leaving a gaping hole for seawater to gush in. Peter figured they would be a submarine themselves in a few seconds.

The submarine had moved about a stone's throw away. A man

pointed to them as they finally emerged from the small boat.

"Over here!" shouted Henrik, waving his hands over his head. Peter and Elise tried to wave, too, but both lost their balance as the deck under them began to tilt even more. But the men on the submarine made no move to rescue them. One studied them carefully through his binoculars, while another gestured. A third man disappeared from sight into the U-boat.

"If they're not going to help us," gasped Peter, "let's untie this boat."

Elise looked at their lifeboat and the web of ropes that held both the cover and the boat in place. "Too late!"

And it was. Only half the trawler was still floating, and it began to twist around, belly up. The thought flashed through Peter's mind that this was the second boat he had seen sink in the past few days.

"Jump!" yelled Henrik.

Peter grabbed for Elise's hand and ran to the edge of the pitching boat. Suddenly, he slipped, and for a moment he thought they would slide backward down the steep deck into the ocean. As another big wave began to turn the craft over, Henrik pulled them higher.

"Now?" Peter looked around at their disappearing platform.

"Now!" yelled Henrik, and together they jumped as far clear of the disappearing boat as they could.

Somehow, Peter didn't feel the numbing cold. He tried to pump his arms and legs as best he could, but it was as if the water had frozen them in its icy grip. Beside him, Elise's eyes were wide with terror. He could feel the suction of the boat ducking beneath the waves for the last time, and a powerful pull as the boat disappeared with a final choking gurgle.

"Swim!" yelled Elise. Peter took a deep breath but only swallowed a mouthful of salty seawater as he slipped down into the green darkness.

Is this what drowning is like? he wondered, choking back the icy salt water. His lungs burned, and his eyes stung as he clawed his way back to the surface. *Up!* cried his lungs as he reached for the dull light above.

In an instant, Peter popped to the top of the waves like a fishing bobber. He gasped and coughed, eager to breathe in the sweet, welcome air. Elise and Henrik were right beside him, splashing and gasping. Now, there was only the sea behind them. The dark shape of the submarine loomed before them.

It was only a few yards away, but it might as well have been miles. Peter could barely make his arms and legs move in the cold. Even if he could swim to the U-boat, he wondered whether the Germans would simply let him drown.

Elise choked on a wave that smacked her in the face as she struggled to look at Peter. "Are you okay?" she panted.

Peter couldn't answer—if he did, he might not have enough breath to take another stroke. He tried to nod and made a sound that sounded something like "uh-huh."

Beside them, Henrik was keeping up, paddling strongly, his dark face knotted into a pained expression. Above them on the submarine, two young men in dark blue pants and baggy sweaters were casually climbing down the outside of the main tower. One of them shouted something over his shoulder, then they both strolled to the edge of the submarine's wide deck.

"How . . . do we . . . get up?" panted Henrik. Even though he was the strongest swimmer of the three, his teeth were chattering, and he was breathing heavily.

Peter looked up at the glistening hull of the submarine. One minute the waves picked them up so they were within reach, the next they were far below. Up and down. One of the sailors waved for them to come closer.

"I . . . can't," choked Elise. Her face slipped under the next wave as it slapped against the submarine's hull and washed back at them. They were close enough to touch it.

With the next swell, Peter felt himself being pulled up against the slippery, gray metal skin of the U-boat. His chest slammed into something hard, and he lost his breath. At almost the same instant, the icy wave dragged him back down, scraping him against the side of the sub. His right foot caught on something sharp, ripping off his shoe, and he was flipped upside down.

"Elise!" he managed to cry. Someone's hand brushed against his, and then everything went black.

WELCOME TO THE U-111

Peter awoke with a moan and struggled to remember where he was. He tried to sit up but bumped his head on a pipe just above him.

"Oh-h," he moaned. His head throbbed with pain, his chest felt as if it had been rubbed raw by sandpaper, and his arms felt twisted and out of joint. Everything ached.

"He's awake," Peter heard a familiar voice whisper. He looked up to see his sister sitting next to him on his bunk, her head stooped. Then Henrik was peering closely at Peter's face.

"Are you okay, Peter?" asked Henrik, looking concerned. "For a minute, I thought you were dead."

"The way I feel, I still might be," replied Peter. He tried to look around, but his neck was too stiff to budge. Everything seemed a little blurry.

"Take it easy, Peter," advised Elise. "You really took a pounding in those waves."

"It sure feels like it, but where are we now?" The submarine. The sinking boat. Getting his foot caught and being smashed by a wave against the rough metal side of the U-boat—it was all coming back to Peter.

"Don't tell me," Peter continued when no one answered him right away. "We're inside the submarine."

"Very perceptive, young man," came a low, scratchy voice Peter had heard before—the voice he had heard on the black boat they had nearly gone down with. Only this time, the voice spoke in accented Danish instead of German.

The man with the skunk-striped beard peeked around Henrik's shoulder. "*Wilkommen*," continued the man. "Welcome to the U–111." He smiled a pearly grin, revealing his gold tooth. "We meet again, it seems. Some of the men wanted to leave you behind. But that wouldn't have been right, seeing as you saved me once. Did you not?"

Peter said nothing but pulled his stare away from the tall man.

"You like my Danish?" asked Skunk Beard. "I was assigned to your capital city, Copenhagen, during the war. Picked up a few words."

"Are you the captain?" croaked Peter. He tried to swallow, but his throat burned, and it felt as if gallons of seawater were sloshing around in his stomach. He wanted to ask why they were in a German submarine, now that the war was long over. But he couldn't get himself to look the man in the eyes.

"The captain?" The man laughed, throwing back his head. "No, he works for me. I'm Doctor Rudolf Wolffhardt, SS. Captain Schulz is back in the *Zentrale*, the control room. We call him the commander. You'll meet him soon enough."

Peter caught his breath at the mention of Skunk Beard's name. It seemed familiar, but he couldn't quite place it. Then he looked at Henrik, and it came to him.

Wolffhardt—the man in the newspaper story about the Nazi treasure!

He knew the others knew the name, too, but he didn't dare say anything.

Dr. Wolffhardt's eyes narrowed as he leaned closer. "First, you're on the tugboat. Then you're out rowing in the fog. Now, would one of you mind telling me what you children were doing on our boat?"

Henrik shifted nervously and looked over at Elise.

"We already tried to explain it to one of your other crewmen," croaked Henrik, "before Peter woke up."

"Yes, of course. But since I'm the only one on this boat intelligent enough to speak Danish, you're going to have to explain it to me." Wolffhardt crossed his arms and looked from one face to the next. Peter closed his eyes, his head pounding like a kettle drum. From somewhere behind them came a steady thrumming of engines. The stench of oily bilge water and diesel fumes stung his nostrils.

"Well, as I was saying"—Henrik swallowed hard—"we were out exploring and thought your boat looked kind of mysterious, and . . ."

Peter opened his eyes to see Wolffhardt staring hard at him, his green eyes blazing.

"Is this boy the only one who speaks?" asked Wolffhardt. The question seemed directed at Peter.

"I . . . I hit my head," Peter tried to explain.

"Yes, I know. Perhaps we should have left *you* behind."

Then Wolffhardt turned his gaze at Elise. "What else?"

Elise's face flushed, and she tried to clear her throat. "He . . . he's right," she finally said. "We were just curious. But when you came back, we got scared. We were so scared that we hid—then someone tied the tarp down on the lifeboat so we couldn't get out."

The man started to nod, a small grin playing on his lips. "Ah yes. I told Dimmlich to do that, thinking the canvas was going to blow away. Of course, he had no idea he was tying three children inside. He's very good with knots. Navy man. Thorough."

Wolffhardt pulled at his beard, as if he was trying to decide something. "Yes, now I see what happened. Three snoopy kids got themselves into a little trouble. Won't their mothers be worried?"

It was Henrik's turn to clear his throat. "Um . . . excuse me, but where are we going?"

Wolffhardt ignored the question. "Yes, your mothers will be *very* worried, won't they?" He seemed to enjoy the idea as he rubbed his hands together with a grin. "But you kids are lucky. We could have left you there in the water, instead of saving your lives. You should be grateful."

To be alive, yes, thought Peter. *To be on a submarine full of Germans who don't know the war is over, I'm not so sure.*

"Grateful," repeated Wolffhardt. Peter couldn't tell if the man wanted them to thank him, or what. But the officer turned on his heel, ducked under a low pipe, and started to leave. Then he remembered something and stopped.

"Yes, of course you're grateful," he answered his own question without turning around. "You're grateful I have a soft heart for children who get themselves into trouble."

When he whirled around to look back at them, his green eyes were flashing. "But you will stay in these quarters here unless instructed otherwise, *ja*? Understand? For the rest of the voyage, you are not to touch anything on this U-boat. *Nothing*—except perhaps the pump toilet in the bathroom. Seaman Apprentice Otto Bohrmann will show you how to use it. He is the young man who pulled you out of the water. He will be along shortly to explain to you about eating arrangements and such."

Wolffhardt pointed his finger at Henrik, as if he were scolding the boy for stealing. "If you hear a buzzer or see a flashing red light, you will stay against the wall, not moving until the all-clear signal is given. Understand?

"We have a long voyage ahead of us. You will be safe—as long as you stay out of the way of the crew and do exactly as you are told. Understand?"

Despite the pain in his neck and head, Peter nodded throughout Wolffhardt's speech. But the man wasn't quite finished.

"If you are caught violating *any* of our regulations, I will not hesitate to place you overboard in the same condition in which you were found. Do you understand?"

Peter knew what condition he had been found in. He nodded again, and Wolffhardt disappeared down the narrow passageway.

"Wow, he's a grouch, isn't he?" whispered Henrik.

Peter said nothing. He was too afraid, and his head hurt too much to nod anymore. He lay back down against his small, flat pillow and looked up at the ceiling.

Elise pulled a gray wool blanket up to Peter's chin. "Peter, you look terrible," she told him. "Your face is green. Just lie down for a while."

Peter tried to smile, but even the muscles in his face ached. "Thanks, sis," he managed to reply.

From his bunk, Peter listened to all the submarine's strange sounds. He could reach the ceiling laced with thick wires and gray pipes without straightening up. Just above his head and to the right, a bare light bulb socket dangled overhead. Every inch of wall and ceiling seemed to be covered with wires, or pipes, or dials.

The constant hum of the diesel engines vibrated Peter's bunk. From somewhere in the boat, men barked commands, echoed by other men who crisply repeated them. Outside were more friendly, familiar sounds—the sound of the waves connecting with the metal skin of the U-boat.

Inside, everything seemed dank and slightly sour, and the rank smell of diesel fumes from the engine seemed to stick to everything—the bedding, the air, even the metal side walls. Peter had smelled something like it once before in a mechanic's shop. But not this strong and sharp. It almost made his eyes sting.

Maybe this is how Jonah felt in the big fish's stomach, thought Peter as he tried to turn around in his cramped little bunk. He knew it had to be late morning by now, but he still felt groggy.

He lifted his head slightly and looked across the narrow walkway to see Elise sitting on her bunk, her arms around her knees. She wore sailor's clothes—dark blue slacks and a baggy black sweater. The same kind of clothes someone had slipped on Peter during the time he had been knocked out. Her eyes looked red, and she started to cry.

"It's okay, Elise," Peter told her, reaching across the hallway to touch the edge of her bunk. But it hurt his arm to move. "Ow!"

Elise looked up in surprise. "Peter, stay still. You're hurt."

"I'm okay," Peter tried to argue. "Just a little scraped up."

"You're scraped up," said Henrik from the bunk below Peter. "And I'm starving."

"How can you think about eating, Henrik?" Elise asked, dabbing at her eyes.

"Don't you remember, Elise?" he answered. "We haven't had anything to eat since lunch yesterday, except for the bread we gobbled on the way to the harbor last night. It must be close to noon. I don't care where we are. I just need something to eat."

Peter felt his friend's head bump him from underneath. His own stomach was growling, too.

Lunch yesterday! They had been back at school in Helsingor for lunch. But now, they were in another world, in the belly of a German whale.

Just then, Henrik's stomach grumbled, and Peter had to laugh at the sound. Elise started to giggle, too, but stopped short when a young teenager came treading down the metal walkway toward their bunks. He wore an outfit similar to theirs.

"*Sprechen sie Deutsch?*" he asked. He looked from face to face, stiffly waiting for an answer. Peter glanced across at his sister. She was better at German than he was—especially at speaking it— but he understood most of what was said. During the war, they had both been required to study German in school.

"*Ja,*" Elise finally answered with a sigh. "I speak German." She was going to have to translate for Henrik, who knew only a few basic words. He had gotten out of taking German when he escaped to Sweden. "But you're going to have to speak slowly."

The teenager grinned at Elise and showed a mouthful of crooked teeth. His ears seemed not to match, the way they stuck straight out. His dark blue pants were rolled up at the ankles, and his brown hair was cut short in a military-style crew cut. Everything about him seemed wrinkled or out of proportion, but he looked friendly enough.

"*Gut*," he replied. "Good. I'm Otto Bohrmann, and I'm supposed to take care of you while you're with us—keep you out of trouble."

Elise introduced herself and the boys, but Henrik interrupted.

"Tell him we're starving," he said. He stood up and pointed to his stomach. "Hungry!" he said in Danish. "Hungry!"

"Does he mean you need something to eat?" asked Otto, looking amused.

"If we're eating, I'm coming," said Peter. Despite his pounding head, he sat up and slid down from off his top bunk. Elise put out her hand to stop him.

"Peter! What are you doing?"

"I'm fine, Elise," he told her, blinking back the pain. "I just need to get something to eat."

The submarine hit a wave and rocked forward, sending Peter flying into Henrik from behind. Henrik managed to grab the side of a bunk while Peter scrambled to his feet. Their guide merely looked over his shoulder, grinned, and said something neither of the boys understood.

"What did he say?" asked Henrik.

"Something about needing sea legs," said Elise.

Once Peter regained his balance, they followed the young sailor down the submarine's narrow main hallway. They stared in amazement at the cocoon of wires and pipes that wrapped around them, all within arm's reach. Dozens of dials, levers, and lights gave Peter the feeling that he was trapped in a science-fiction movie. There was hardly room to turn around.

"Hold on," Henrik called back as the boat pitched again.

"I am," answered Peter. Odd smells swirled around his head, and his stomach was starting to feel strange. With the fog of damp diesel fumes, the air in the submarine was like that behind a bus during a rainstorm. The rocking motion was so strong Peter thought he could probably move faster if he crawled.

They passed three or four rows of identical double-decker bunks, all neatly made, before reaching another section of beds. These were different; each one tucked into a small cubicle. They were a little nicer, some decorated with black-and-white photos of what looked like wives and girlfriends. Many had small shelves over the bunks jammed with dog-eared books. But all the bunks were strangely empty. The group still hadn't seen anyone.

Up ahead, Peter could hear men's voices, and someone was arguing hotly.

"I tell you, I didn't sign up on this trip to be your galley slave!" someone complained. "I'm a torpedo operator, not a cook."

"Yeah, sure," came Wolffhardt's unmistakable voice. "We don't have very many torpedoes on this trip, but we do need to eat."

"Fine, but who put you in charge? I think the commander ought to make work assignments, not you."

Wolffhardt's voice grew cold. "Listen, sailor. Things have changed, or haven't you noticed? You're not in the navy anymore. I'm in charge now, not your pitiful commander. He can get us to where we're going, but I'm writing the checks for this trip. Understand?"

"Sure, but—"

"*I'm* the one who stuck his neck out. *I'm* the one who rescued the treasure. I just need your help to get it to a safe place, then everyone will get a share. But just because the cook got himself captured before we left doesn't mean we're going to starve. With less than half a crew aboard, we will all have to do a little extra work. Understand?"

There was another grumble from the unfamiliar man up ahead, and then Peter and the others stepped out into a small kitchen area. Otto stopped at the front of their line and turned around.

"This is the galley," he said, sweeping his hand around the

small compartment. It was half the size of their little kitchen at home in Helsingor, but there was a small stove, two ovens, and three hot plates, a short refrigerator, and a stainless-steel sink with three faucets. In the corners of the small room hung cloth bags with sausages poking out the top, and Peter almost tripped over an open crate of apples. Hammocks of hard pumpernickel bread swung dangerously near their heads, threatening to hit anyone who wasn't careful.

Elise looked at the sink curiously, touching one of the faucets.

"Hot, cold, and . . ." she wondered softly.

"Hot salt water," finished Otto. "We use it for many things, even cleaning. We have a machine that makes a little fresh water out of the salt water, too." He said it as though he was quite proud of the boat. "But there's not enough water to shave with, even though we have only twelve men on board. The Old Man won't let us waste water. And if you've ever tried to shave with salt water, you won't try it again. Hurts!"

Peter looked at the teenager's chin, obviously untouched by a razor. Otto looked too young to know much about shaving.

"Usually, we have forty men on this submarine," Otto continued. "Twelve is a skeleton crew—hardly enough to run a U-boat. Everyone has to work two or three jobs."

While Elise translated for Henrik, Peter looked around the cramped room and wondered how they could ever fit forty men into such a crowded space.

"It's cramped," admitted Otto. "But you get used to it. As long as you don't sit up too fast in your bunk, you'll be fine."

Otto was about to take them through the galley when another man came storming into the room from the opposite direction. Behind his blond beard he was red in the face, and he was muttering.

"We need someone with your experience," said the man, mimicking someone else. The man continued muttering as he shoved Peter to one side, leaned into a cupboard, and pulled out a pot. "This Wolffhardt character's never been on a submarine in his life, and now all of a sudden he has all the answers. So what does he do? Tells me to cook soup!"

The stocky little man with enormous, muscled forearms straightened up and seemed to notice for the first time that others were in the galley.

"Why don't you kids run along and play?" He glared at them.

"This is Petty Officer Helmut Bockstruck," said Otto, a grin playing on his face. "He's supposed to be in charge of torpedoes, but Wolffhardt made him head of potatoes, instead."

Helmut picked up a long, wooden spoon and was about to hit Otto in the head. But he seemed to think better of it, and instead stood for a moment looking at Peter, Elise, and Henrik.

"What are these stowaways doing to earn their keep, Otto?"

Peter looked nervously at his sister. He was willing to work so they could eat, but there was no way any of them would help shoot torpedoes. Especially not if this sour-tempered Helmut fellow was in charge.

Otto just shrugged. "Don't know yet. I was just taking them up to see the Old Man and find out what I should do with them. I'm kind of confused, though. Who's in charge, the commander, or Wolffhardt?"

"That's what I'd like to know," growled Helmut. "But look— I'm supposed to cook three meals a day for more than a dozen people, and I don't know the first thing about cooking. I could burn water, and I doubt anyone else on this insane trip knows any more about cooking than I do. But now it looks as if we have three kids who can take over for me."

"I don't know," answered Otto reluctantly. "I'll have to ask. . . ."

"Ask nothing. Just tell the Old Man they're working for me. I'll keep them out of his way."

Otto nodded and motioned for Elise, Henrik, and Peter to follow him. Henrik grabbed an apple on the way out.

"Hey, kid!" roared Helmut. "That's for later. Put it back."

Henrik looked back, puzzled.

"He said to put it back," translated Elise. She turned to Helmut and tried to smile. "His German isn't very good," she explained.

"Ja? Well, we'll fix that," retorted Helmut, picking up a potato peeler. Reluctantly, Henrik replaced the apple in its crate.

"Hey, Helmut, how about it?" Otto asked. "We *are* going to feed these people, aren't we?"

Helmut looked up and pointed his potato peeler menacingly. "Ja, they can eat with everyone else. But they missed lunch, and dinner is at four. No special treatment." He paused for a moment and frowned. "All right. If they're that hungry, give them a slice of bread and a sausage. Just this once."

The man turned to fiddle with the small stove as Peter, Elise, and Henrik devoured their sausage sandwiches. Peter washed his down with several glasses of fresh water. Nothing had tasted so good to him in a long time.

"Know what else?" complained Helmut. He didn't wait for Otto to reply. "Half the labels on the food cans are gone. That's right, the labels are gone. So how does anyone expect me to fix a meal if I can't even tell what's in a can?"

Otto started to giggle.

"You think it's funny? Do you want me to make beef stew with a can of apples?"

Otto just kept laughing. Peter didn't know whether to join in or leave.

"All right, all right." Helmut finally shooed them out of the galley. "If anyone finds out I've been letting you kids have snacks, the entire crew will start stealing food. Get out, now."

Peter tucked one last crumb into his mouth before he followed the others out of the galley and down the long main hallway.

"No sense of humor," Otto told them. "But Helmut is okay. Wolffhardt, though, you had better watch out for. No one trusts him. Especially not the commander."

The next section of the submarine seemed different than the forward compartments they had come from. There were four private bunks in this larger room, two on each side. The walls were oak paneled, and a cupboard contained porcelain dishes and cups. The cream-colored overhead lampshades looked like something they had in their living room back home—quite a change from the wire-covered bare light bulbs they had seen in the rest of the submarine.

"Wait here a second," whispered Otto, walking over to where Dr. Wolffhardt sat at a linen-covered table with a large, bearded man. *He has to be the commander*, thought Peter. As Otto whispered something, the man looked up at them from his plate of sausages.

"So, these are our stowaways," he observed, wiping his mouth with the edge of his white cloth napkin. He looked straight at Peter. "Your names?"

Peter forced himself to speak under the commander's withering stare. "I'm Peter Andersen," he croaked. "This is my sister, Elise, and my friend Henrik Me—"

Peter bit his tongue, remembering that Henrik's last name sounded very Jewish.

Here we are on a German submarine, and I'm telling these people my friend is a Jew! The German navy is supposed to hate Jews!

"My friend Henrik," Peter corrected himself with a cough. *Maybe they won't care about last names.*

"Yes, very well," replied the commander, chewing another mouthful of sausage. "I'm Commander Karl Schulz of U-boat U–111. I believe you've already met Seaman Bohrmann." He waved his fork at the boy. "I will relay any instructions to you through him. You will be assigned to galley duty for the remainder of this voyage. That is all."

He stared at them for a moment, sending chills up Peter's back. There was ice in the man's penetrating blue eyes, and what could be seen of his face behind a neatly trimmed beard was pockmarked and scarred. There was no doubt that he was in charge. Peter held his breath when he heard Henrik clearing his throat.

"Uh . . . excuse me, Herr Commander," began Henrik. Peter

flinched, afraid of what would come next. Henrik worked hard to put together the right German words, but he was obviously having trouble.

"Could you . . . uh . . ." He turned to Elise. "Elise, ask him where we're going, would you? I get some of what they're saying, but I can't put together sentences."

Elise swallowed nervously but nodded.

She's brave, thought Peter.

"Henrik would like to ask where we're going," Elise explained.

Peter looked to see the commander's surprised expression.

"Our destination, young man," replied the commander, carefully delivering his words, "is none of your concern. Do you understand my German?"

"Did he say it's none of my business?" Henrik whispered to Elise. She nodded.

"You and your friends are here as guests of the German Reich only because of the mercy of the crew of the U–111," the commander continued. "You will perform your duties without further questions until instructed otherwise. You will be let off this ship when—and if—it is convenient for us to do so. Do I make myself clear?"

He dismissed them with a sweep of his fork. Dr. Wolffhardt, who had said nothing all that time, finished his meal with a smirk.

"Oh, Commander, one other thing." Otto held up his finger.

The commander raised his eyes, his mouth full of sausage.

"Would it be all right if I showed them around the rest of the boat?"

"Quickly," the commander warned. "This isn't a cruise ship. I take it you've warned them to stay out of the way? To touch nothing?"

"They know," Otto assured him. He motioned again for Peter, Henrik, and Elise to follow.

Otto stopped just outside the officers' area next to two small rooms on the left side of their hallway. Both were filled to the ceiling with exotic-looking electronic equipment. In the first, a slim, pale-looking man with sunken cheeks sat with earphones facing a glass-covered compass and a control wheel. He didn't look up when they stopped by his cubicle, only seemed to stare more intently at his compass.

"That's Gunther Gabl," said Otto. "He's our sound man. And on this trip, he's doing double-duty as our radioman, too. He speaks a little Danish from listening so much to the radio."

Gunther waved his hand in a swift greeting, still not taking his eyes from his compass.

"Aren't those the same job?" asked Peter. "Sound man, radioman?"

"Oh no," Otto responded. "They're usually two different jobs. We just don't have a real radioman on this trip. But Gunther can do the job. From here, he can hear everything. Propellers from miles away, ships, other subs, even whales and dolphins."

The man in the heavily paneled sound booth spun the wheel on his instrument panel and leaned closer to his compass. Elise tried to translate most of what Otto was saying for Henrik.

"Hear anything?" asked Otto.

The man shook his head. "The usual shipping. I'll be glad when we get farther out into the ocean." Then he pulled off his earphones, pushed out his little chair, and stepped around the corner to the radio room next door. They all followed.

"This is different from the sound room," Otto explained as Gunther snapped on a transmitter.

The radio room was twice the size of the sound booth, and it was crammed with even more electronics.

"Morse code key?" asked Peter, pointing to a small switch with a black handle.

"Ja," replied Gunther. "Morse code." He pointed to several other instruments in turn. "Transmitter there. Receivers. Code machine. Record player for playing music."

Elise noticed the neatly labeled collection of thin black disks the size of small pizzas. They were stacked sideways in brown cardboard holders under the counter.

"What kind of music do you play?" she asked.

The radioman shrugged and frowned. "The Old Man likes Wagner. Opera. Large women with Viking helmets who sound like foghorns. And there's some Italian opera, as well. We play it down below when the water is calm and the records don't skip. Or sometimes we listen to the radio news, but there's not much point, anymore. It's all bad news."

Elise looked disappointed. "Any Jimmy Dorsey?" she asked. "Bing Crosby?"

The man looked surprised. "*Nein.* No swing-band music. No popular singers like Crosby. And *never* Americans."

By then Peter and Henrik were leaning closer, trying to see what Gunther was doing with one of the larger receivers. Black and shining, it stood almost as tall as a small refrigerator and was covered with heavy knobs and dials. Gunther had all the dials lit to a soft orange glow.

"What's this machine?" Henrik asked cautiously in Danish.

"This is a transceiver," answered Gunther, leaning back in his chair so the boys could get a better look. He was obviously proud of his radio. "It both sends and receives. The finest radio in the fleet. We installed it just before the end of the . . ." He paused. "Just a few months ago."

"So you could talk to someone in Germany with this?" asked Peter.

Gunther nodded, then frowned. "We used to. Now, there's no one left in Germany to speak with."

"Then what's it good for?" Peter wanted to know.

Gunther almost laughed. "Nothing. All I do is listen in on radio messages from ships in our area to hear what they're saying and where they're going. Right now, it's just a lot of *English.*"

The way the man spit out the word "English" made it very clear that he wasn't very fond of the language. Probably not of anyone who spoke it, either.

Peter studied the radio carefully, trying to understand the writing beneath the dials and the settings. "Is that what you're doing now?" he asked. "Listening to ships?"

"Ja."

"And what's that for?" Peter continued, pointing at what was obviously a microphone.

"Microphone, of course. But we don't use it anymore. As I said, we have no one left to talk to."

"But it still works?" Peter was afraid he was asking too many questions, but he had to know. And the man seemed to speak passable Danish, almost better than Wolffhardt.

"Ja, but . . ." The radioman's expression clouded over, as if he realized he was talking too much. Shaking his head, he waved them off and switched back to speaking German. "But this is no business of yours. Enough questions."

"Come on," said Otto, pulling them along. "And stay out of the radio area. It's off limits for anyone but Gunther and the officers."

Peter thought he heard a crackling English voice coming from the radio's loudspeaker. He could barely make it out.

"Let's keep moving." Otto gave Peter a serious look. "It's my job to keep you three out of trouble. And here's another place you must stay away from."

He turned them toward the other side of the hallway, directly facing the sound and radio rooms. A heavy green curtain hung in front of them.

"Is this the shower?" asked Elise.

Otto was about to pull back the curtain but stopped and laughed. "Shower? You asked if this was the shower?"

Elise pulled back, puzzled. "No?"

Otto couldn't stop laughing. "There are no showers on a German submarine."

"That explains the smell," Henrik mumbled after Elise told him what Otto had said.

Otto looked suspiciously over his shoulder. "What did he say?"

Henrik held his nose, and Otto nodded. "He'll get used to it. But this isn't the shower—it's the Old Man's room." He pulled back the curtain to reveal a tiny, oak-paneled living and working space. There was barely enough room for someone to turn around next to a small bunk, a locker, and a washbasin tucked underneath a hinged writing table.

"The only private room on the ship," explained Otto, holding the curtain back so they could see. "Besides the bathroom, that is. And by the way, there are two of those. One forward and one next to the galley. I'll show you how to pump the toilet."

"We know how," volunteered Peter. He thought of some of the small ships he had been on. But Otto only shook his head.

"It's not the same as what you've seen," he said. "If you don't pump it right, it works backward. I guarantee—"

"Okay, we understand," interrupted Elise. "But what about extra clothes, or a towel? And does anyone have a brush?"

Otto gave her an amused look. "A brush? That's pretty funny. You think we'd have a brush on board?"

"I was just wondering," stammered Elise.

"You're lucky we have only a skeleton crew. There's a big pile of extra clothes and things in the forward end—stuff that got left on board by earlier crews. You're wearing some of the clothes now. Some of them are even clean."

While Otto rambled, Henrik inched forward, curious to see the desk. Otto held out his arm to stop him. "I told you, this is the Old Man's room. They'll fire you out through the torpedo tubes if they ever catch you in there."

Henrik backed away, a puzzled expression on his face.

"The Old Man?" asked Elise. "You keep saying that. Who's the Old Man?"

Otto laughed again. "You kids don't know anything, do you? That's what we call a submarine commander. Ours might be mean, but he's had to be to survive three years of war duty in the

North Atlantic—the best commander in the German fleet." The young teen's eyes took on a faraway look, and he swallowed hard. "The only commander left."

"What do you mean, he's the last commander left?" Peter asked carefully. He already knew the answer, but he wanted to hear it from a German. Otto faced him, his chin up defensively.

"Don't you people know the war's been over for a month?" continued Elise. "Ever since May 5. And why can't you tell us where we're going? Is this some kind of secret mission?"

For a moment, Otto hesitated, and Peter thought he saw him soften. "I can't . . ." began the teenager. Then a hardness fell over his face, and he straightened up. "You will do exactly as the commander ordered," he droned, turning his back to them. "And I cannot answer any more questions."

He jerked the green curtain closed, stepped away from the commander's room, and led them on through the hall. "Now, as we come into the Zentrale, you will remember to touch nothing."

9

COMMANDER TO
THE BRIDGE

"Wow," whistled Peter as they stepped into a room full of even more dials, levers, and pipes. "I've never seen anything like this."

He leaned back to take in the sights of the control room, only to see a framed picture of the dead German dictator, Adolf Hitler, in a place of honor on the wall above a row of dials. Henrik looked up, too, and scowled.

"This," began Otto, pointing to a ladder in the middle of the room, "leads upstairs to the conning tower—the way you entered the submarine. But you must not touch the ladder without permission."

Peter and the others nodded nervously. Along the wall, two sailors stood watch over their massive collection of instruments. Several more were upstairs on the observation deck; their laughing and chatter filtered down through the open hatch above Peter's head.

"The Zentrale is the control center of the finest submarine in the German submarine force." Otto assumed his proud look.

Peter gaped in wonder at the maze of controls. "Does the commander know how to work everything?" he wondered aloud.

Otto leaned casually against a pipe and shook his head. "Not the commander. Only the chief knows every control on the sub. He watched it being built a couple of years ago, so he knows it inside and out."

"Who's the chief?" asked Elise.

"Chief Max Weiss, the first watch officer. He's second in command behind the commander. And he's usually on bridge watch." Otto jerked his thumb at the ceiling. "We're not supposed to go up unless we have special permission from him." He leaned forward, as if he was about to tell them a secret. "But I might be able to get you up there if you're lucky."

Peter frowned. *How can we possibly be "lucky" when we're trapped in a German submarine with this crazy crew? Are they just pretending the war isn't over?* he wondered. *How could we have gotten into such a mess?*

"We cruise on the surface as much as we can," Otto was explaining. "That way we can use our diesel engines. They need air to run, of course."

"Do you work with the engines?" asked Peter. He had noticed Otto's black fingernails and dirty-looking hands. And instead of trim, light-brown pants, Otto wore smudged, dark-blue work clothes—like a mechanic's coveralls.

"Ja," answered the teenager. "I help keep the engines running." He pointed to the back of the Zentrale, where another door led to the engine rooms.

"What happens when we dive?" Elise translated for Henrik, who had been following the conversation with her help.

"You'll find that out soon enough," answered Otto. "We have both diesel and electric motors. We run on batteries underwater. But only for a day or two, tops. We have to come up for air sometime."

Otto was about to lead them out of the Zentrale when a voice came booming out of an open copper tube on the wall.

"Commander to the bridge!" barked the voice.

A moment later, the commander came jogging into the room and disappeared upstairs like a monkey up a tree. He now wore a white-topped officer's hat.

"Why does he wear a white hat when everyone else wears blue?" Henrik asked.

Elise turned to their young guide. "Henrik wants to know why the commander wears a white hat."

"Tradition," Otto replied. "And it also makes it easier to tell where he is outside in the dark."

The commander was gone less than a minute before he reappeared, sliding down the ladder fireman-style ahead of two others. They each hit the metal grating of the floor with a thud and scurried to their stations.

"Stay there!" Otto barked at them as he disappeared into the engine room. "Don't move, and don't get in the way."

Peter, Elise, and Henrik huddled in the corner of the control room, their eyes wide. Peter glued himself to the wall and tried to blend into the maze of pipes and wires.

"What do you think's going on?" he whispered to Elise.

"Maybe they saw something," she suggested. "A ship, maybe."

Above their heads, the last man pulled the hatch cover closed and spun the steering-wheel-sized latch shut.

"Tower watch secured, Commander," noted the man as he slid down the stairs. His boots hit the metal grate with a loud slap. "The bridge watch is below."

The commander studied a set of gauges over a seaman's shoulder. "Very well, Chief," he said coolly. "How far away is the ship?"

"A safe distance," answered Chief Weiss, an intense man in his midthirties. "We have plenty of time to dive." Like everyone else on the submarine except for Otto, he wore a beard. Peter thought the man looked like an aristocrat, but his eyes were as wild as an animal's.

"Then take us down to periscope depth," the commander ordered. "E-motors one-quarter speed. Dive!"

The chief responded instantly, slamming his fist down on a large button. "Flood negative!" he shouted.

Peter jumped when he heard the loud buzzer repeat the call to dive. Large red lights overhead blinked in time to the buzzer. It seemed that everyone in the submarine was calling out commands and counter-commands, and the radio intercom in the control room crackled with activity.

"Air vents open," came a voice over the speakers. "One, two, three, four, five!" A great hissing sound told them the float tanks had opened to let out air and let in water. Soon they would be sinking.

Dr. Wolffhardt hurried into the Zentrale, wiping his mouth with a napkin.

"What's going on here, Schulz? Why wasn't I called in?"

Commander Schulz didn't even look up. "Go back to your sausages, Wolffhardt. You're in the way."

Wolffhardt stood there, his cheeks puffing and his face red. "You are going to regret your sharp tongue, my dear commander."

"Flood valves open!" came another report. Peter felt a lurch as tanks somewhere in the front of the submarine took on sea water. Commander Schulz continued to ignore Dr. Wolffhardt, who stood for a moment, glaring and tight-lipped, before turning and disappearing the way he had come.

"Diesel air valve closed! Diesels shut down and disengaged!" The rumbling in the background fell silent, leaving only the sounds of shouting men, hissing air tanks, and bubbling water. Then the electric motors began to hum.

"E-motors ready, one-quarter speed!" reported a voice from the engine room.

The chief leaned over and spoke to two men who sat on bicyclelike seats. They were in charge of a set of strange-looking buttons with hand grips.

"Forward down ten," he told them. "Aft down five. Let's take her down easy."

The two men pressed button after button and wrestled with the control wheels, all the while watching a set of gauges. Peter guessed from what the chief had said that their job was to keep the submarine balanced.

"Keep us in a steady dive," he told one. "Not too steep."

Until then, Peter had hardly dared breathe, but he began to relax as the activity slowed. Then one of the men in the bicycle seats started calling out numbers.

"Ten meters," he informed the chief. "Eleven, twelve, thirteen, thirteen and a half . . . periscope depth."

The dark-haired chief looked around at the control room crew. For a second, he glanced at Peter, Elise, and Henrik, still unmoving in the corner. He wrinkled his brow in a slight frown but said nothing.

"Forward up three," he commanded. "Aft up three. Close air vents and flood valves. E-motors slow ahead. Ready to level out."

"Slow ahead," came an echo from the engine room radio.

Finally the chief turned to Commander Schulz, who was bent over the large chart table in the other corner. "We're trimmed and stable, Herr Commander," he said. He wasn't smiling, but something about his eyes told Peter that the man was happy with the way his boat had responded. "Would you like a look?"

The commander glanced up from his charts with an absent expression. "No, not now, Chief. I have to remind myself that we're not hunters anymore. Just keep the periscope in the well. But increase to three-quarter speed. We have just eleven hours to make our rendezvous point."

The chief's face fell, but he nodded obediently. "Yes, Herr Commander."

Henrik took a step out and glanced curiously at the chart the commander had been studying. The commander turned to the kids, as if noting them for the first time. Henrik instantly faded back into the wall with Peter and Elise.

"Where is Bohrmann?" asked the commander. He looked straight at Henrik but seemed to be talking to someone else. "Tell Bohrmann to get these stowaways out of my hair while we're diving. I'm going back to finish my lunch."

Peter tried to back even farther out of sight and out of the way as the chief pulled a microphone off its cradle on the wall.

"Seaman Bohrmann to the Zentrale." The chief's tinny, nasal voice made a buzzing echo over the loudspeakers positioned throughout the ship.

A sudden hissing sound, like air escaping from a balloon just behind him, made Peter jump. Otto came scurrying up to the control room, wiping his greasy hands on a dirty rag.

"I told you not to touch anything!" he shouted at Peter, who jumped. Otto quickly reached to shut off a valve that had opened when Peter had accidentally leaned on it.

"Let's get you back to your bunks," directed Otto. He put out his hands like a mother hen and herded them through the Zentrale and the officers' quarters, through the galley, and back along the narrow hallway to their bunks.

"Now, stay here until Helmut is ready for you in the galley."

"Excuse me," said Elise, putting up her finger shyly. "But you said something about getting some extra clothes?"

Otto gave her an annoyed expression but nodded. "Up forward on the port side, just before the torpedo rooms. You can't miss it. There's a big stack of things. Take what you want. Everyone else has already been through it."

Within a few minutes, Elise had found the pile of clothing and towels. "Look at this, Elise," said Peter, holding up a couple of blue sailor's shirts. "Will any of these fit us?"

Elise held one up to her face and sniffed. "At least they're not dirty. We may have to dress like German submarine sailors, but we don't have to smell like them."

Henrik grinned at his friends and dug through the pile of shirts and pants. "Hey, there's even clean underwear!" he exclaimed.

"Henrik!" Peter scolded. But Elise ignored them.

"Here's what I was looking for," she said quietly, digging down through the pile and unwrapping a brown paper parcel. "Toothbrushes, combs, soap . . ."

"Doesn't look like many sailors took a pack," observed Peter.

"They must be care packages from home," Elise said, reading the German writing on the package. "There's a woman's name here—from Hamburg. A women's aid society sent this."

Henrik gave a little bow. "Well, thank you, women's aid society."

Peter made a duffel bag by tying knots in the ankles of the largest pair of pants he could find, stuffing everything inside, and tightening the top with a belt. "There," he told the others. "Everything I need. Two wrinkled blue shirts. One lumpy sweater. Three pairs of pants, soap, a comb, and a toothbrush."

"We'll use baking soda from the kitchen to brush our teeth," said Elise, looking closely at the only other comb she could find. "I sure hope this thing is clean."

"Didn't it come wrapped in the care package?" asked Henrik.

"Yes, but . . ." Elise made a face as she tried to run the comb through her tangled hair.

"Hey, you three!" yelled someone from behind them. Peter startled at the sound and stared behind them down the narrow hallway. Helmut, the torpedo man, stood with hands on hips, frowning. "Are you about done here?" he growled. "I need some help in the galley before dinner."

10

GALLEY SLAVES

"Here," growled Helmut Bockstruck when they reached the galley. He pointed to a pile of sprouting potatoes in a large bucket. "The girl can wash them in salt water and peel them. As for that one," he pointed his chin at Henrik, "tell him he can get busy washing those leftover lunch dishes."

Peter was left with the task of scrubbing down the counters and cleaning several large kettles caked with burned food. Helmut, in the meantime, turned his attention to a paperback book and settled down on a stool in the corner.

"Where do we put these when we're done?" asked Henrik, holding up a plate. Helmut mopped his brow and grunted in the direction of a cupboard. Peter sighed and scrubbed harder at the hopelessly crusted food on the bottom of the pan; it looked like a combination of ancient oatmeal and cheese. The submarine crew obviously hadn't had much time to wash dishes. *At least the water is hot*, Peter told himself, dipping his hands deep into the sudsy water.

The warm water was about the only thing that seemed to fight the chill clinging tightly to everything in their damp, underwater world. Peter closed his eyes for a minute to soak up the warmth.

"How are you feeling, Peter?" Elise whispered in his ear.

Peter pulled his hands out of the suds. "Every bone in my body aches, but I'll survive."

"Here, Peter, catch!" said Henrik, acting as though he were going to throw one of the plates.

"You two, knock it off!" commanded Helmut. "You have work to do."

And they certainly did. For dinner that night Peter and Elise were drafted as waiter and waitress, serving both the officers and the crew their meal of steaming hot potato soup and bread. But on his way out with the first serving of soup, Peter paused to inspect the contents of one of the bowls.

"Elise, what's in this soup?"

Elise looked at the two bowls she was carrying. "I don't know. I thought it was just potatoes. But you're right—there *is* something else in here."

Peter smelled the soup, then carefully fished out what looked like a small, limp piece of black rubber. He smelled it, then nibbled the corner.

"Oh," he groaned. "This isn't just potato soup. This is *prune* potato soup."

They looked at each other, and Elise shook her head. "Helmut told us he didn't know what was in those cans, but I didn't think—"

"Hey!" yelled someone from the wide spot in the hallway just past the Zentrale where the crew took their meals. "What happened to dinner?"

"Coming!" Elise called back. They hurried to the folding table where some of the crewmen were sitting, set down the bowls, and hurried back to the galley.

"Amazing," Peter remarked as they picked up another load. "I don't hear anyone complaining."

"And for dessert," announced Helmut, clearly not hearing Peter's comment, "we'll serve the crew's favorite—chocolate pudding. Of course, without fresh milk, it tastes a little different. But pudding it is."

Henrik was put to work in the kitchen, ladling refills of soup. The men, amused with their new galley help, kept the twins running back and forth with request after request for more soup, more bread, and more to drink. It seemed to Peter that the sailors purposely asked for just one item at a time.

"Hey, hurry it up," roared one of the men, a big, blond fellow in his twenties. "Where's my pudding?"

Peter had seen him in the Zentrale during the dive, working some of the controls. He wasn't positive, but he thought it was the same man who had come aboard with Wolffhardt. When Elise slipped over to the crew's fold-down eating table to see what he needed, the man grinned at her.

"Ja, this is all right! Does she shine shoes, too? Maybe with her hair?" He grabbed at Elise's hair, but she managed to escape. Two of the metal plates she was carrying slipped from her hands, clattering to the floor.

"Leave her alone, Dimmlich," snapped Otto, noticing Elise's red face. Peter turned red, too—but from anger rather than embarrassment.

"What did I do?" replied the sailor. "I'm just having a little fun. She's pretty clumsy, though."

"Just leave the kids alone," replied Otto, putting down his fork and getting up from their small crewmen's table. "Commander Schulz doesn't want any trouble."

"Oh, so now I'm getting lectures from the boy who doesn't shave yet, am I?" Dimmlich drew himself up to face Otto. He was a head taller and many muscles heavier.

"Listen, Dimmlich, I don't want any trouble with you." Otto stood his ground. "Let's just forget it."

Two other men joined in.

"Yeah, forget it, Dimmlich," said one.

"It's not worth it," added the other. "They're just clumsy little kids."

Peter and Elise tried to slip back to the galley without being noticed, tiptoeing through the Zentrale on the way. But Peter's foot caught as he stepped through the round hatch leading out of the control center, sending his trayful of dirty dishes flying. Behind him, Peter could hear a chorus of laughs.

"Pretty good waiters we got there," said a man, sounding amused.

Helmut looked down the hallway from the galley.

"What's going on out there?" he asked, frowning viciously. "Do you kids have a problem holding on to your dishes?"

On their hands and knees, Peter and Elise quickly gathered the plates, and Peter mopped up a puddle of spilled soup. He wasn't able to catch all of it, though, since it had spilled down through the see-through metal grating of the floor to the dark, damp area below. He hoped no one would make him go down there to clean up the rest.

"No problem, sir," replied Peter. "We're just bringing them back."

"Well, bring them back in one piece if you can manage it," barked Helmut.

Peter didn't know where he least wanted to be—in the galley, or back with the jeering crew. He looked over at Elise and saw the tears in her eyes. "It'll be okay," Peter whispered as they gathered their last plate and headed back to the galley.

Elise just nodded, wiped her nose, and looked straight ahead.

"Next time I send you back for dishes, I expect you to come back without making a mess," growled Helmut the minute Peter and Elise walked into the cramped kitchen area. They nodded.

"Hear me?" Helmut crossed his arms, still holding a large soup spoon.

"Right. Sorry," apologized Peter.

The man frowned. Peter wondered how he could be so crabby, considering he was getting so much help. But he knew better than to say anything.

"All right," continued Helmut, looking around the galley.

"We're out of rye bread in here." He pointed his nose at Peter. "You fetch some. It's up forward, just past your bunks. Understand?"

Peter thought he did, so he nodded. At least Helmut was speaking slowly.

"All right, then. You'll find some cloth sacks of bread hanging on the starboard wall. Just bring back two sacks."

Peter nodded again and disappeared as quickly as he could, slipping down the hallway past the lower officers' cubicles, then past his own bunk in the forward end of the submarine.

As he neared the forward torpedo rooms, he could see through the opening of a white-painted, round, metal bulkhead door that stood open. Against the side walls were two shiny torpedoes, each one about twenty feet long, painted dark gray, and secured by heavy straps. Peter thought of what they could do and shivered.

The torpedoes were surrounded by crates of food, baskets of oranges, and cloth sacks full of the black bread German sailors seemed to live on. Peter bent over to take one of the bags but bumped into a bag of oranges. A half dozen spilled out, hit the floor, and rolled into a corner under the torpedoes.

"Oh no," he whispered to himself, crawling around the crates and chasing the runaway oranges. "If they roll down below, I'll never reach them."

Peter couldn't see under the torpedo, but he managed to retrieve two of the oranges right away. Then he heard a squeak in the far forward end of the room, and he looked up just in time to see the red wheel handle spinning to open the forward compartment door. Out of instinct, Peter crouched low in the shadows. He peeked out from behind the sack of oranges just as Dr. Wolffhardt stepped through the door.

The man chuckled softly, pausing to shut the door behind him. As Peter watched silently, Dr. Wolffhardt spun the wheel handle shut and popped an extra-heavy padlock on a latch that Peter hadn't noticed before. Then the man turned to face Peter's direction, holding a shiny coin up to the bare light bulb overhead. He smiled and flipped the coin into the air.

"Ha," Wolffhardt said to himself. "There's another year's salary that the commander doesn't need to know about."

He carefully replaced the coin into his pocket before walking down the corridor, never noticing Peter huddled behind the food. When Peter was sure Wolffhardt was far enough away, he uncurled from his hiding place and grabbed two bags of bread. *Now I know where they're keeping Henrik's treasure*, he thought as he stepped back into the hallway. *Not that I care anymore.*

———

Helmut finally let them return to their bunks at eleven that night after hours of dishwashing and pan scrubbing. The German officer seemed to get a special satisfaction out of having Peter, Elise, and Henrik clean each pot twice. And if he found any spot on the cookware, they had to polish it until it sparkled. That done, they were given a large pile of brass belt buckles to shine.

"I like it," said Helmut, grinning at his reflection in the side of a stainless-steel bowl. "Gut."

By the time Peter made it back to his top bunk, he was ready to fall asleep anywhere. Elise hung a sheet from the bunk above hers for a little privacy and crawled into her homemade tent. Henrik flopped on his cushion on the bunk below Peter. Peter's eyes were shut even before he hit the flat pillow.

"I think we had to clean up dishes that have been dirty since before the war," moaned Henrik. "But at least we weren't anywhere near Wolffhardt."

"I saw him," said Peter, not opening his eyes. "Along with more of your treasure."

"No kidding?" Henrik's voice brightened.

"Yeah. He was coming out of the front torpedo rooms, and he had a gold coin like the one we found. He locked up the treasure behind him."

"So he's keeping it all up there?"

"Has to be. There aren't many other places to hide the boxes we saw them loading from the boat."

"Hmm." Henrik grew quiet for a moment. "Not that it matters, but I learned something, too. I know where we're going."

Peter didn't want to respond, he was so exhausted. He pulled his blanket up over his shoulders to fight off the damp, bone-chilling air.

"Where?" Elise's teeth clattered as she peeked out from behind her sheet.

"Holland. I saw it on the commander's map."

"Are you sure?" asked Peter doubtfully. "Why would we be going to Holland?"

"Look, I don't know." Henrik sat up on his bunk and bumped Peter from below. "All I know is that I saw the commander's map, and there was a line drawn right off the coast of Holland—and a big X."

"That doesn't make any sense," said Peter.

"Maybe it does," said Henrik. "It makes sense if they're going to Holland to get rid of some of their treasure. Maybe sell it."

"Hmm." Peter frowned again. He tried to roll over, but his back was still sore. It made him nervous to know that the Nazi treasure was just a few yards away from where they slept.

"Maybe we can escape when we get closer to land," Elise suggested. "Did you see how close the X was to shore?"

"I couldn't really tell," Henrik admitted. "You think we should try to swim for it? But how? They won't even let us outside."

"That *is* a problem," sighed Elise.

"Henrik," Peter asked. "Do you still have that coin?"

Henrik reached into his pocket and pulled out the glimmering gold piece. "I've had my hand on it all day. If we could only figure out how to get into that locked room, we—"

"Henrik," interrupted Peter. "We need to get off this smelly submarine, not find more treasure!"

"Peter's right," agreed his sister. "This place is creepy."

"Hey, I didn't mean anything by it." Henrik pushed up on the bottom of Peter's canvas bunk. "I just thought that since it was so close . . ."

"I don't think we should risk it," Peter finally said, flopping back on his damp pillow. "Let's get some sleep. Aren't you tired?"

Almost too exhausted to pray, Peter held himself awake for just a moment longer. It didn't matter to him that the hallway lights were still burning. Apparently, the lights were kept on day and night.

"Good night, Jesus," he whispered into his pillow. "Help Mom and Dad not to worry too much about us. Please don't let Wolffhardt find out that Henrik is Jewish. And, Lord, please don't forget us down here."

DESTINATION HOLLAND

"What were we doing last Sunday at this time, Peter?" Elise asked the next morning as they were washing breakfast dishes. No one else was close enough to hear them, and Henrik was in the officer's wardroom gathering more dishes.

Peter had to think for a moment. It already seemed so long ago.

"It doesn't seem like this is Sunday morning at all," he told Elise, swirling a dish in the water. "Not without Grandfather and church."

"I know," she admitted with a sigh.

Elise smiled a little, and Peter imagined they were back home in Helsingor, washing the breakfast dishes. Of course, Elise looked a bit different wearing blue sailor's pants and a large blue shirt with rolled up sleeves. Still, she looked a lot better in clean clothes and with her hair pulled back in a ponytail than Peter and Henrik did with their rumpled clothes and wild hair that pointed in all directions.

Peter tried to remember the Bible verse their grandfather had quoted as they were walking to church just a week ago. And it occurred to him what he had been missing during the past few days: his Bible.

"Remember that verse Grandfather told us?" He tried to pull back the memory. "Something about how chasing riches is useless . . . like chasing after the wind—"

"Hello there," interrupted Otto from behind them. "Good breakfast. How's it going?"

Peter closed his eyes and didn't turn around. For just one more second, he wanted to keep pretending that he was at home. He would happily wash the dishes forever, if only it weren't here on this cold submarine.

"I said, how's it going?" the teenager repeated.

Peter shrugged, and Elise whispered a quiet "fine."

"I just thought I'd let you know," continued Otto. "We're returning to the surface in a couple of minutes. You might want to finish your dishes before the waves start knocking us around again."

Peter looked over his shoulder and caught Otto's eye. *Maybe he's truly trying to be nice,* he thought. *Maybe he's stuck here like us. Maybe he's not like the other Germans.*

"Thanks," Peter forced himself to say. "And . . . uh . . . thanks for sticking up for us last night at dinner."

"Sure." Otto lifted his chin slightly. "It was nothing. The crew is always acting tough. You just have to know how to handle them."

Henrik returned and dumped a stack of dishes on the narrow counter by the stove. He picked up one of the dishes and twirled it over his head.

"Coming in for a landing!" he announced, flying the plate past Peter's head. He started to laugh, then stopped short when he finally noticed Otto. He returned the plate carefully to the sink.

"Oh, him again. What's he doing here?"

"He came to tell us we're going to the surface," answered Elise.

Henrik stared at the teenager. "Where are we going?" he

asked him in Danish. Otto just looked confused and turned to the twins.

"I said," repeated Henrik, this time louder, but still in Danish, "WHERE ARE WE GOING?"

"He's asking where we're going," repeated Elise in German, looking down.

Otto didn't answer right away, but his grin turned to a frown. "You'll find out soon enough," he finally told them. "I have to get back to the engine room."

With that, Otto turned on his heel, took a few steps, and stopped. He reached into his pocket for something and wheeled around.

"I found this under your pillow," he told Henrik, tossing a small silver chain at him. Then he looked at Elise. "Tell your friend he should be more careful where he keeps his Star of David. Most of the crew don't give a fig about Jews, but Wolffhardt would kill him if he found out."

Then Otto disappeared. Henrik just stood there, looking at the small necklace that identified him as a Jew.

"What did he say?" asked Henrik nervously. Elise told him, her voice trembling.

"I didn't even know you wore that," said Peter, not knowing what else to say.

"I took it off as soon as we got here. It's my dad's."

Henrik started to walk out of the galley but came face-to-face with Helmut.

"Oh," said Henrik, startled.

Helmut ignored Henrik and pointed seriously at the stack of dishes. His double chin bobbed when he spoke.

"Finish quickly, now, and then stack everything so it won't fall. We're surfacing in four minutes." Then he turned to Henrik, held up four fingers, pointed to his watch, and jerked his thumb at the low ceiling. "*Vier Minuten*. Four minutes. Understand?"

Henrik nodded and picked up a towel. Helmut's sign language was plain. Henrik dried while Peter scrubbed the officers' dishes double-time and Elise rinsed. True to the man's prediction, three minutes later they heard urgent commands from the Zentrale. The floor lurched beneath them.

"Lookouts to control," ordered the commander over the loudspeakers. Four sailors dressed warmly with blue sweaters and wool caps came hurrying past them in the hallway. Even though it was summer, it was still cool out on the ocean. A moment later, they could hear commands again, this time without the loudspeakers.

"Standby to surface," the commander barked. "E-motors down to three-quarter speed. Steer up."

The floor tilted up like that in a carnival ride. Peter set the last dish in its place in the cabinet next to the sink.

"Blow out main ballast. *Surface!*"

Peter edged out into the hallway, closer to the Zentrale.

"Bow up twelve, stern up ten," ordered the chief. Bubbles rushed past them inside the walls, swirling noisily through the pipes overhead.

"Ten meters . . . seven . . . five. Conning tower clear," one of the men reported.

With that announcement, men raced up the ladder. A blast of fresh, cool ocean air found its way in as the hatch was finally popped open.

"We're on top again," Peter told the others.

"Where do you think we are?" asked Elise, drying her hands on a dish towel.

"Holland." Henrik sounded sure. He grinned and gave them a thumbs-up sign.

"I'd like to see for myself," said Peter. Even though they had only been in their tin-can world just over a day, the outside air smelled wonderful. The thought of seeing land sounded pretty good, too. "Think they would let us up?"

There was more shouting from the control room.

"Both engines full ahead," Commander Schulz directed.

"That means that everything's clear up there," grunted Helmut.

They turned around to see their "boss" leaning up against the wall with his usual sour expression.

"Clear?" asked Peter.

Helmut frowned even more. "If the Old Man had seen anything, he would have pulled the plug real quick."

"You mean we would have dived again right away if there had been anyone else up there?" asked Elise.

"That's what I mean." Helmut leaned his shoulder into the wall as the ship began to sway again with the waves. The sensation was so different from the steady, quiet stillness down below.

"Steady on course o-nine-five," shouted the commander from up above. "We'll make the coast by nightfall if we don't run into any enemy shipping."

Peter looked over at Henrik and whispered, "Hear that, Henrik? Holland by nightfall."

Dangerous Rendezvous

As morning turned to afternoon, Peter and Elise started to get used to the feel of the waves again. In between galley chores, they found some cards and tried to occupy themselves playing card games like Old Maid. Just like at home, Elise usually won.

Henrik, however, paced in front of Peter's bunk, where the twins sat playing their games. Every time someone walked by, he had to squeeze to the side to make room.

"Are you okay, Henrik?" Peter finally asked. "It's been a while since we've heard a joke from you."

"Joke?" Henrik looked up as if he hadn't understood. Then he smiled. "Oh . . . I'll think of something—don't you worry." He paced off in the opposite direction.

"Peter, don't push him," Elise whispered.

Peter looked up from his cards. He had the Old Maid—the Queen of Hearts—in his hand. But it was Elise's turn to draw a card. She still might take it.

"I'm not trying to push him. I just miss the old Henrik, that's all."

"Yeah, but you have to admit, being trapped in a U-boat isn't funny. He's probably worried about his dad. Can you imagine what would happen if Mr. Melchior heard his son was missing?"

"I hope he doesn't hear. But Mom and Dad probably had heart attacks, too. They must be going crazy worrying about us."

"Well, what do you expect? We disappear, just like that. I wish there was some way we could get a message to them . . . maybe over the radio."

Peter shook his head. "Too risky. Gunther Gabl is always sitting in the radio room. And someone would overhear us if we tried."

Henrik stopped pacing and raised his finger. "Okay, how about this for a joke," he began. "Why do German submarines always sink?"

Peter looked around to make sure no one else was listening. "I give up. Why?"

"Because they forget to close the screen door!" Henrik grinned, waiting for someone to laugh.

Elise giggled and Peter smiled. Henrik stepped aside again when the sound of footsteps approached from the back of the boat.

"It's Otto," he reported.

"Don't tell *him* your joke," warned Elise.

The teenager strode up with a grin on his face.

"I got permission from the commander for us to go topside a little later," he told them. He looked at Henrik and pointed at the ceiling.

"We can go up the ladder?" Henrik turned to Elise for an answer.

She nodded, and Otto held up his finger in warning.

"You three are lucky the Old Man's in a good mood. But just one at a time. And only if you promise to stay out of the way."

Peter wasn't sure why Otto was acting so friendly. Was he trying to be their friend? *Why is he doing this for us?* he wondered.

"Meet me in the control room after you finish the dishes," said Otto as he turned to go. "Eighteen-thirty."

Peter was used to the military time the sailors used. He didn't have to do any math in his head to know that eighteen-thirty meant six-thirty that evening.

"Let's get the dishes done quickly," said Elise, her excitement showing in her voice.

Peter nodded his agreement, even though something in him didn't trust Otto. Still, the chance to slip out of their cold, gray metal world sounded good. Very good. And the thought of breathing fresh sea air . . .

"No problem, Elise," Peter replied. "We'll have those dishes done in forty-five minutes."

———————

Peter and Elise fidgeted nervously as they stood off to the side of the Zentrale. Henrik was studying a mysterious-looking gauge that seemed to indicate how deep under the water's surface they were. All needles pointed to zero.

One of the sailors watching the instruments on the other side of the control room gave Henrik a dark stare. Henrik pulled his hands back and held up his palms.

"Don't worry," he mumbled. "I wasn't touching anything."

Just then a voice crackled over the loudspeakers. "This is the new *Deutchlandsender* on wave band three-hundred-sixty meters . . ."

"Ah." The young sailor broke into a smile. "There's still a radio station in Berlin."

"And here is a little dance music," continued the announcer, "the popular dance tune, '*Es War in Schönberg im Monat Mai.*'"

"I was in Schönberg in the month of May," repeated the sailor, a slender man in his twenties. "That's a neighborhood in Berlin. Been there before?"

Peter and Elise shook their heads no.

"Berlin's where I'm from," said Otto, stepping into the control room. He stopped for a moment, as if remembering a better time. "Beautiful city." He shook his head, and his expression clouded.

"Or at least, it used to be. Before the war and all the bombing."

"Does your family still live there?" asked Elise.

"Wolffhardt said my parents escaped before the war ended," he replied. "I'm going to see them again at the end of this trip. They're waiting for me in South—"

The talkative teenager caught himself in midsentence and glanced around the quiet control room. No one seemed to be paying attention; the nearest sailor had left to check some instruments on the other side of the room. Otto shrugged. "They're waiting for me in South America. That's . . . well, that's all you need to know. Who's going up first?"

"South America?" asked Peter. "You're going to South America?"

Otto ignored the question. "I said, who's going first?"

All three looked at one another. Peter raised his eyebrows at Elise. "Ladies first?"

But Elise shook her head. "No, one of you boys go first. I'll go next."

"Go ahead," Peter told Henrik. "He says we can go up one at a time. I'll wait."

"All right," announced Otto in his more serious tone. "Tell your friend the rules I told you, or it's the last time you'll get fresh air. Stay out of the way and stay quiet. Do as you're told. Ten minutes, and then let someone else have a turn."

After Elise had repeated Otto's instructions, Henrik winked at them and hurried up the ladder after the teenager. While they waited, Peter and Elise gazed up at the soft, golden light coming from the open hatch. The air smelled wonderful, even from below.

"I'll be back," said Henrik, waving at them with his foot and disappearing up through the hatch.

A long ten minutes later he was back, and Elise looked nervously up at the conning tower.

"What's the matter, Elise?" asked Henrik. "It's real nice. No one else is there besides Otto and the commander and two crewmen with binoculars. I did get the impression the commander isn't too thrilled about us being up there, though."

Elise shook her head. "I don't want to go up there by myself."

"Why not?" asked Henrik.

"I just don't."

"I'll go with you," Peter volunteered.

"Otto said only one at a time," protested Elise.

"They won't mind," Peter decided. "There's probably plenty of room up there."

So Peter followed closely behind his sister as they carefully climbed the ladder. At the top, Otto looked at them curiously. He was standing on the edge of the observation platform—it reminded Peter of the Kronborg Castle tower where they had once watched ships.

"Does it matter if we both come up to get some air?" asked Peter, choosing his words carefully.

Otto glanced over at the commander, who narrowed his eyes a bit, looked around at the open ocean, and nodded slightly. He pushed his white hat back off his forehead. "Five minutes, then."

Peter looked around at an ocean the color of deep pink-and-gold roses. The sun was setting, and a low, gentle swell pleasantly rocked the U-boat. Even the low clouds above them took on the color of the sun.

"Pretty," Elise told her brother as they leaned out over the railing.

"Almost nice enough for a sail," agreed Peter, thinking back to their little boat in Helsingor.

Elise nodded. She looked around at the three men standing on deck as they constantly scanned the horizon with their binoculars.

"Where's the land?" Peter asked Otto.

Otto nodded off ahead of them at a low bank of clouds. Peter didn't dare ask anything else, but he knew it had to be Holland. It was much too far away to even dream of swimming.

After a few minutes, the men's voices grew louder. The commander sounded irritated, and he kept looking at his watch. Finally, he turned to his copper speaking tube.

"Send Dr. Wolffhardt upstairs," he commanded, sounding reluctant.

A voice from below gurgled a reply, then a moment later Wolffhardt clattered up the ladder. He didn't appear to notice Peter and Elise.

"They're not here, Wolffhardt," commented the commander, lowering his voice to a whisper and pointing to his silver wristwatch. Still, Peter could make out a few words. "Can't wait . . . more," it sounded like.

Wolffhardt mumbled something back to the commander, grabbed a pair of binoculars from one of the sailors, and scanned the horizon himself. No one said a word for several more minutes. Peter didn't say anything, either, afraid the commander would remember they were still there and chase them downstairs. Finally, Wolffhardt grunted in disgust and turned around. He seemed startled to see Peter and Elise in the far corner of the platform.

"Where did these kids come from?" he asked the commander. "Who said they could come up here?"

Otto stepped forward. "The commander said it was all right."

Wolffhardt's stare seemed to drill holes in Otto. He lunged forward and grabbed the teenager by the front of his sweater, his red-rimmed eyes bulging as they went toe to toe.

"You better watch your mouth, boy," he hissed. "And take our *guests* below where they can't get in the way. Understand?"

"Wolffhardt!" interrupted the commander. "Let go of him. I'll make those decisions."

Wolffhardt reluctantly let go of Otto's sweater and glanced over his shoulder. "Surely you don't want—"

"I said *I'll* make those decisions. You've done it to us again— we're deep in enemy waters, and your friends and their boat aren't here. I'm taking us out of here now while we still have our skin. This place is crawling with enemy shipping."

"Listen, Karl," protested Wolffhardt. "There's a lot more at stake here. Just think: Your own ranch in Brazil, a car, servants— it's more of a retirement plan than the military ever offered you."

"We have enough to live like that now," snapped the commander. "The torpedo rooms are full to the ceiling with enough treasure to make us all rich men for many lifetimes. Now if you don't mind, we're through here. Clear the platform."

"You're making a mistake, Commander," insisted Dr. Wolffhardt, his voice rising in anger. He faced Commander Schulz now, his fists clenched in rage.

"A mistake?" the commander almost shouted. Peter thought a fistfight would break out any moment. "The only mistake I've made is calling you up here. Get out of my sight!"

But before Wolffhardt could reply, one of the lookouts sounded a warning.

"Commander!" he called. "Two planes dead ahead, heading straight for us."

"What?" replied the commander, grabbing the binoculars back from Wolffhardt and searching the direction the lookout had indicated.

"They just dropped out of the clouds, sir." The lookout tried to apologize, but Commander Schulz didn't give him a chance. In the distance, Peter could hear the whining of an airplane's engine.

"Down, down!" the commander ordered. "Everyone down below!"

The commander shouted into his speaking tube as everyone slipped down the ladder in a practiced panic. Peter felt Otto push him from behind, and he half fell, half slid down to the floor. His palms burned from gripping the ladder too tightly. At the bottom, the Zentrale had become a beehive of activity and shouting. Henrik, however, was nowhere to be seen.

"Dive!" the commander shouted. "Hit the cellar fast! All non-essential personnel to the bow!"

"Come on!" said Otto as he slid down behind Peter and Elise. "Run forward!"

Peter had no idea what was going on, but he grabbed Elise's hand, and they both shuffled forward as fast as they could, Otto pushing them from behind. The buzzing of the dive siren was so loud they could hardly exchange shouts, but they managed to make it down the hall, past their bunks, and all the way forward to the door Peter had seen Wolffhardt exit the day before. Henrik was waiting by the white door.

"*All* the way forward!" commanded Chief Weiss over the loudspeakers. Peter could hear him as clearly as if he were standing right next to them. "We need more weight in front!"

Wolffhardt hesitated in front of the door, but Helmut rushed up behind him.

"You heard the chief," said Helmut, spinning at the wheel of the round door handle. "Open it up. We have to get our weight all the way forward immediately, or we may not make it down fast enough."

Wolffhardt planted his feet firmly in front of the locked door and shook his head.

"Wolffhardt!" shouted Helmut. "Now's not the time to worry about your treasure. If we don't get down fast enough, your treasure will be lost—and so will we."

Finally, Wolffhardt seemed to pull together. He pulled a key from his pocket, unlocked the door, and threw it open for the others to pass through. Peter tried to follow them inside the compartment, but the powerful man put out his hand to stop him at the door.

"You and the girl will wait out here." He looked at Henrik, who was standing behind Peter. "Him too." Then he ducked back into the forward compartment and disappeared.

Peter didn't have time to wonder. The submarine dipped down once more, only much more steeply this time. Peter held on to a pipe overhead as everything began to slide across the floor at them.

"Watch out for those boxes!" he yelled, but he was too late. A wooden crate of potatoes slid across the metal floor and right into Elise's legs. She fell over the top, spilling it and sending potatoes all over the floor.

"Elise!" cried Peter, grabbing for her arm. He missed and fell on top of her as the U–111 sank nose down with a loud hissing and bubbling. For a moment, the overhead lights dimmed, then blinked off and on. Peter could hear Wolffhardt fussing in the forward compartment.

"No one touch a thing," he ordered. "Not a thing!"

Peter held his breath, as if doing so would help them to sink faster. But then he caught himself. He didn't *want* them to sink faster. "Maybe we should have jumped off while we had a chance," he whispered to the others. *We could have done it,* he told himself. *Maybe the planes would have seen us.*

But then, he thought, maybe they wouldn't have. The past two days since they had hidden on the black trawler had been a nightmare, but at least they were together and safe for the moment.

"Aren't they dropping depth charges?" asked one voice in the forward hold.

Peter strained to hear, though he wasn't quite sure what they were listening for, or even what depth charges really were.

"Level out at thirty meters," came the commander's voice, sounding cool and in command even over the crackling loudspeakers. "We're checking upstairs to see if anyone is following."

Sitting on the floor, they waited fifteen tense minutes, then thirty. After a while, a few of the men began to return to their posts. Smiling and joking, they filed past Peter, Elise, and Henrik. Elise was still rubbing her shins where she had been hit by the crate.

"You're going to have a big bruise there," Peter told her, taking a look. "But I thought I was the only one who's supposed to get bumps and bruises."

Elise nodded but said nothing. Her eyes were brimming with tears.

A minute later, Otto stepped out of the forward hatch with a grin.

"Didn't I tell you the Old Man could get us out of any trouble?" he asked.

"What was happening?" asked Elise.

"Wabos."

Elise looked back at him in confusion.

"Wabos," repeated Otto. "*Wasserbomben.* Water bombs. Depth charges. They're dropped out of planes or ships, and they explode underwater." He clapped his hands together for effect. "That's how we lost so many other subs. But not the U–111."

Another sailor squeezed past them.

"Next stop, Rio," he told Otto, doing a little dance.

"Quiet!" scolded Helmut, bringing up the rear of the line. "You know what the commander told you."

Now Peter was sure where they were going, and he looked at Henrik and Elise to see if they had heard. Neither of them looked up, but their serious expressions told him everything. They knew.

Later that evening, the submarine surfaced while Peter and the others were relaxing on their bunks. The fresh salt air felt good as it found its way into the cramped submarine. It was a touch cooler this time, though.

"I bet they'll never let us upstairs again," Henrik said aloud as the engines came to life. "Do you think?"

"Not after the scene Wolffhardt made when we were on the deck with Otto," Peter answered. *Just as well*, he told himself.

A couple of minutes later, the lively German music pumped over the loudspeakers told them that the commander was more relaxed. The seas were all clear.

Pretty soon, though, the music changed to a newscast. A rather worried-sounding German voice began reading the events of the day. Peter could tell Elise was listening carefully, and he tried to catch everything the man was saying, too.

"The last of the once-powerful fleet of German U-boats has been destroyed by Allied naval forces," droned the voice, "as over one hundred surrendered U-boats were towed into the North Atlantic and sunk. At the end of hostilities in May, several dozen were intentionally sunk by their German crews in a final act of defiance. According to the Allied command, only two U-boats are still missing, the U–238 and the U–111. Both are thought to have been sunk during the final days of the war, although a Royal Dutch Air Force patrol reported seeing an unidentified submarine a mile off their coast. All efforts to reach the submarine have failed."

The crew cheered at the mention of their own submarine. Even Helmut grinned as he walked by their bunks.

"Ha!" he cried. "So they saw us, did they? Well, the others may have given up, but I'll tell you one thing: The U–111 still has a couple of torpedoes left to fire! And when I'm firing those eels, we don't miss."

The chief came up behind him just as Helmut was giving his speech, and the weapons officer now turned cook stopped short. The chief looked straight at Helmut as if to scold him, then grinned slightly.

"I'll let you know if we have need of any torpedoes, Herr Bockstruck," the chief told him. "Just remember what our mission is this time."

Helmut snapped to attention, obviously embarrassed that the chief had seen his eagerness to continue fighting. "Absolutely, Chief. I just meant that if there's ever a tight situation where you need a torpedo officer, you can depend on me, sir."

"I know what you meant, Helmut." The chief's icy personality seemed to melt a few degrees. "We all feel the same way. We're the only ones left, remember? U–238 was hit and sunk off Norway—only the English never realized it."

"Yes, sir. I knew that."

Peter tried not to stare, tried to pretend he wasn't paying attention to what the two men were saying.

But the nightmare was real. Hearing it on the radio had made it seem even more so. He, Elise, and Henrik were trapped on the last German submarine, heading for South America with a torpedo room packed full of treasure. By now, their parents probably thought they had drowned somewhere. And Peter was stuck washing dishes next to a man who was eager to fire torpedoes at anyone who stood in their way.

13

Secrets

"You'll get used to it," Otto told Peter a couple of days later as Peter fell limply into his bunk. It had been another exhausting morning of chores. "I get all the dirty work in the engine room because the crew thinks I'm just a kid. Anyway, we only have a couple of weeks before we reach our destination."

"Rio de Janeiro?" Peter lifted his head. Henrik and Elise would be back any minute.

"So you figured it out. I guess it wasn't much of a secret."

Peter nodded. But he still hadn't figured out everything. Why was Otto working on the submarine in the first place? He tried to phrase the question in understandable German, but he wasn't quite sure of the words.

"Why," he began, then faltered. *Where is Elise?*

"Excuse me?" asked Otto.

"Where—" Peter tried again but was interrupted by steps coming down the hall. It was Elise.

"Boy, am I glad to see you, Elise. Could you ask Otto why he's a part of this crazy crew? He's so young."

Otto listened to Elise ask Peter's question. For a second, he looked as if he would paste on his stern expression, but instead he softened.

Otto glanced around. No one else was in the hall. "I started helping on submarines last year because the German navy needed people to fight," he began. "My older brother was killed on a submarine—I wanted to get back at the British."

Otto's eyes looked misty, but he shook his head and went on.

"I was on the U–160 for a few months, then they transferred me to this boat. I may be young, but I'm good with engines." He clenched his fists. "And then, well, the German navy surrendered.

"Except for Commander Schulz," he continued. "He's swell— lets me up topside all the time. He rounded up all the crew members left in Germany one night, and we slipped out of Kiel Harbor—right under the Allies' noses! 'Karl Schulz does not raise a white flag!' I heard him say. At first I didn't want to come, but then he told me he'd help me find my parents once we get to Rio. He and Wolffhardt said they escaped to Brazil during the last days of the bombing."

Elise stared down at the floor as Otto finished his speech. Peter couldn't look at Otto, either. And there was something else he was wondering about.

"What about Wolffhardt?" Peter asked.

"Wolffhardt?" Otto looked quickly up and down the hallway as if he were about to tell them a secret. "Stay away from Wolffhardt. He's the one who put this whole trip together, but he's half crazy."

Otto lowered his voice. "He's a doctor, but not for sick people. Some kind of art expert. Bockstruck told me he worked directly for Hitler, collecting all the art treasures of Europe. If you haven't figured it out already, the treasure is why everyone is on this submarine, except me. Wolffhardt told the crew we would all get part of the money from the sale of the treasure once we make it to South America. Me? I just want my share—then I'm going to find Mom and Dad."

Mom and Dad. As Otto went on, Peter leaned against the wall, closed his eyes, and tried to imagine what his parents were going through. By now, they would think that Peter, Elise, and Henrik were dead. Or would they? Grandfather's little boat was safely tied up. They had just vanished. He wished he could slip into the radio room and send them a message. Something, anything, to let his parents know they were okay.

Lord, he prayed quietly, *isn't there some way you can tell them we're okay? And isn't there a way to get off this horrible submarine before we get to South America?*

"Hey, Peter, wake up," came Otto's voice.

"Huh? What?" Peter cleared his head with a jerk. Otto was staring straight at him.

"He wants to know if we would like to go topside again," explained Elise.

"Oh . . . I . . . uh . . ." Peter wasn't at all sure he wanted to go up where they might get shot at again—although fresh air did sound good.

"I do," said Henrik. He had appeared from somewhere down the hallway. "Remember, Peter, when you told me you wanted to see the world? This is our chance."

"Well?" Otto asked again without waiting for an answer. "I know you want to. I'll go check on it right now. We should be surfacing again tonight, I think."

Peter, Elise, and Henrik followed along behind Otto as he went to find the commander. Just past the galley, they stopped in front of the sound and radio rooms, across from the commander's quarters. Inside his room, the commander sounded irritated, and Otto held up his hand for them to stay back.

"Are you sure, Gunther?" asked Commander Schulz.

"Absolutely, Commander," answered the sound man. "It sounds to me like the propeller of a British or American destroyer. Maybe even a group of aircraft carriers. Ever since we left Holland, it's been chasing us. It's on the far edge of what I can hear, but it's there, sir. I'm sure of it."

"All right. When we surface a little later, we'll keep a close watch for the ship. At least we know what direction to look."

"But unless it gets closer, sir, we won't be able to see it, especially if it gets dark. It's still too far away."

"Understood. But right now we don't have a choice. We have to surface to charge the batteries. If we don't, we won't make it to Brazil."

"I'll keep listening, sir."

"Keep me posted."

"Yes, sir."

With that, the commander stepped out of the sound booth and turned immediately toward the Zentrale without giving the group a look.

"I better not ask him now," whispered Otto. "Looks as if he has his hands full."

Peter nodded and backed up. He tried not to show it, but the thought of a British or American ship following them sounded like an answer to prayer.

Later that afternoon, they did surface, and this time the boat started heaving and tossing as never before.

"What's going on?" asked Elise, trying to keep a pot of cabbage cooking on the stove. She hung on with one hand and stirred with the other while the pot threatened to slide right over the little railing wrapped around the stove.

"Just weather," Helmut informed her as he headed for the Zentrale. A sailor was coming down the ladder, his black oilskin rain suit and tall rubber sea boots dripping.

"No ships in sight, Commander," Peter heard the sailor report, "but we're having trouble hanging on. The chief made us wear safety belts. Seas are getting higher all the time."

The sailor was right. Even from the galley, they could hear the wind screaming above them. And since they were on the surface, they could feel themselves climbing larger and larger waves all the time. Once Peter looked up through the conning tower to the open hatch, but all he could see was white spray.

"Here's a big one," said Henrik, holding on with both hands to the counter in the galley. They climbed what must have been a giant cliff of water, then hung in midair for a moment before plunging down the other side of the wave. The nose of the submarine dug in, its back end following with a slap that sent shivers through every metal bone of the giant ship. All around they could hear the twang of the impact, like a concert of steel springs. And then they repeated the dance as they began the climb up another giant hill of water.

After one particularly hard thump, a sheet of cold salt water came pouring through the open upstairs hatch. Peter heard the men down below in the Zentrale yell and complain.

"Shut the hatch up there," yelled one. "We're getting a shower."

But Helmut only laughed and stuck his head out into the hallway. "You fellows could use a shower," he told them.

"Go back to your cooking," they shouted back.

After a few more minutes, Elise had to give up on dinner. There was no way to keep anything on the burner—and even if they could, the food was spilling all over the kitchen.

"Looks as though we'll be serving bread and cold sausages again," said Helmut.

Peter groaned to himself. The bread wasn't bad, but he was sick of the fatty German sausages they had already eaten for several meals. The men never seemed to tire of them, though, so he set to work slicing enough meat to serve the first round of crewmen. After Peter had loaded a metal plate with food, he started down the main hallway, stopping every two steps to grab on to a pipe. Finally he made it to the sound room, where the commander was huddled next to the radio operator with one of the earphones pressed to his ear.

"I don't hear it, Gunther," the commander said, handing the earphones to the other man. Peter tiptoed slowly past the door, hanging on to the wall with every step.

"It's all the wave noise, sir. I heard the sound for a while before we surfaced. Now I don't hear it, either."

Both men hung on with both hands as the sub tilted almost sideways, then upright, then over like a clock pendulum swinging to the other side. As the craft started to climb another wave, the commander noticed Peter hanging on in the hallway.

"Hey, boy," he told Peter. "Let's see that food."

Peter nodded nervously, holding out the plate of sausages and bread. But just then the submarine dipped over the wave, and the plate slipped out of his hands, dumping the food in a heap on the commander's feet.

Peter could feel the commander's angry glare as he got down on his knees and picked up as much as he could. By then, half of the sausages had rolled into the corners of the room and out into the hallway. The sound man reached down, grabbed a sausage off the floor, and took a big bite. But the commander didn't move.

"Sorry," Peter mumbled as he crawled back out into the hall. He tried to make it back to the galley on all fours.

"Did you serve all that food already?" Helmut quizzed him when he returned to the galley.

"Sort of," Peter replied. Henrik and Elise were picking up silverware from the floor and trying to stuff what was left into two small cabinets. Elise looked as pale as Peter had ever seen her.

"Are you okay?" Peter whispered to his sister.

"Uh-huh," replied Elise. She didn't look okay. Her eyes were doing cartwheels.

"This is nothing," Helmut assured them, leaning against a wall. "Two winters ago we hit a storm in the North Atlantic, force twelve at least. We were stuck in that horrid hurricane for ten days before it calmed down. Lost three men—washed away."

"Why don't we just go down under the water where it's calm?" asked Elise, bending over and holding her stomach.

"Oh, we will a little later," replied Helmut, helping himself to one of the rescued sausages on Peter's plate. Peter didn't have the nerve to tell him where it had been rolling. The torpedo man kept

talking with his mouth full of sausage. "But we can't run on batteries for more than fifteen hours or so, depending on how fast
we push. We always have to go back up to recharge the batteries.
Besides, the E-motors—the electric motors—are too slow." He
shoved the last bit of sausage into his mouth. "Any bread left?"

Peter nodded and gave him a piece from his plate.

After another hour of crawling around the pitching ship with
bread and sausages for the crew, Helmut gave Peter his final assignment for today.

"Bring this up to the watch crew, would you? They get hungry
up there."

Peter looked down at the plate of food. "Um, you mean up on
the observation deck?"

"That's what I mean. Or should I repeat it to you in Danish?"

Elise stepped up to Peter's defense. "Can't they eat when they
come back down?"

But Elise's resistance only set off Helmut's temper. "Listen.
You kids have had an easy time up until now. If you don't want
to work, though, I can arrange a lot more pain for you. . . ." He
looked straight at Peter, a dark glimmer of anger burning in his
eyes.

"I'll go," Peter replied, snatching the plate out of Helmut's
hands. The chubby man chuckled.

"Be careful, Peter," Elise urged him.

Henrik looked on in total confusion. "Where's Peter going?"
Peter didn't think he should take the time to answer.

By the time he reached the Zentrale, the submarine was buck-
ing and dipping even more than before. Several times Peter was
thrown to his knees, but he managed to keep the plate steady.
With only one hand for balance and one to hold food, he had no
idea how he was going to make it up the ladder. One of the sailors
on duty looked over as Peter put his foot on the first step of the
long ladder up—or sideways, depending on which way the boat
was rocking.

"You're not going up there, are you?" asked the sailor, looking shocked.

Peter nodded and took another step. "Helmut told me to." He gripped hard with his left hand, swallowed, and looked up into the tunnel leading to the closed hatch.

The ladder felt slippery to the touch. But if he timed it just right, Peter found he could make it up two steps between waves, then hold on for a minute while the submarine went through its twisting and turning. Then two more steps, then hold on. Five minutes later, he was looking at the hatch, thinking that he needed an extra pair of hands to open it.

Peter finally wedged his shoulders in under the hatch and hooked his left elbow around the last step up. With his free left hand, he gripped the plate of food, and with his right, he spun the wheel handle to the hatch. Then he straightened his shoulder and pressed with all his strength on the metal lid, praying it would open.

Opening the hatch turned out to be the easy part. Just as Peter nudged it up an inch, the storm wind reached in and flipped it open with a slam. He was almost sucked up by the force of the hurricane, his head flipped back like a puppet on a string by a blast of salt water.

Even though the back of his head smarted from the blow, Peter knew he couldn't just stand there. He lifted himself up out of the hatch into the early evening grayness, scooted up on the slippery deck, and tried to get on his knees. But before he could even get a grip on a railing, a wave washed over the conning tower, soaking him to the skin. Somehow he held on to the plate and found a railing to grab with his free hand. He pulled himself to his feet and looked straight into the rain-suited figure of the chief.

"Who told you to come up here?" yelled the chief over the sound of crashing water and wind.

"Herr Bockstruck," Peter replied. "He told me that you wanted some food up here."

The chief gave Peter an incredulous stare. "That's the most foolish thing I've ever heard." The wind whipped the words from the man's mouth.

Peter heard a muffled shout from behind them and turned around—just in time to see a wall of gray water, marbled with white strips of foam, rising over the submarine.

The boat started to climb backward up the enormous mountain of water, then shuddered halfway up as the top began to break over them. Peter knew he had only a moment before they would be buried in cold seawater. He dropped the plate and wrapped both arms around the handrail beside him.

If this is how you want me to die, God . . . he prayed, but he didn't have a chance to finish as the wave buried them.

Peter felt his body swept up in the force of the water as his feet flapped out to the side like a flag in a hurricane.

I'm not letting go, he told himself, even though the wave had nearly yanked his shoulder out of joint. His eyes bulged in pain.

Suddenly, the submarine bucked as the wave washed past them almost as quickly as it had come. Peter rolled around on the deck, finally letting his aching arms release the rail. He glanced up at the handrail and closed his eyes. It was hanging on by a single screw.

"Everyone all right?" shouted the chief.

They glanced at one another in the half darkness. The other men had managed to hang on—or rather, their safety harnesses had held on to them. They rose to their feet, sputtering and shaking. The chief pointed his finger at Peter and shook his head angrily.

"Get below before you get yourself killed!" he shouted. Peter wasn't about to argue.

Without another word, Peter slipped back down through the hatch, half falling to the floor of the control room. The hatch slammed shut above him.

Once at the bottom of the ladder, he shuddered as he thought about the wave that had nearly swept him into the stormy sea.

He was sure the men on the submarine wouldn't have tried to save him, even if they could have. And he was sure God had held the last screw on the handrail.

"Peter, are you okay?"

Peter looked up and saw Elise struggling down the hall, her face wrinkled in concern. "That big wave . . ."

"I'm okay," Peter replied, his voice shaking.

"You may be okay," said one of the sailors on watch. "But we're getting wet in here from all the water you let in. And your stupid plate almost hit us on the head."

Peter looked down at the floor of the Zentrale and saw the steel serving plate he had worked so hard to carry up the ladder. It had been scrubbed clean by the salt water. He wanted to kick it as far as he could, but instead he bent over, picked it up, and returned with Elise to the galley. Helmut was waiting with a smirk on his face.

"Got a little wet, did you?"

Peter reached over and dropped the plate into the sink with a loud clatter. He knew why the German had sent him up into the storm. *He's probably disappointed I made it back*, he thought.

"They didn't want the food," he told Helmut.

Helmut shrugged and kept his pretend smile on his lips. "Oh well," he said. "You tried. Take a break."

Elise put her arm around Peter's wet, aching shoulders and helped him down the hallway to their bunks. While Henrik found him something dry to wear, Peter leaned against his bunk, shivering. Another wave hit, and the boat shuddered once more.

"Don't you think Mom and Dad will figure out somehow where we are?" Peter asked quietly, choking back the tears. He didn't want to cry. But every time he thought about where they were and how far away from home they must be, he almost couldn't help crying.

"Maybe," whispered Elise. "Maybe."

But Peter knew the answer was no.

14

FRIENDS FROM THE DEEP

The stormy weather dragged on for the next week, leaving the crew irritable and tense. Even Elise, who tried to look her best by washing her hair every other day in the galley sink, was looking pale. Her usually perky cheeks seemed a little sunken and drawn as she worked in the galley with Peter and Henrik.

The only good part, thought Peter, was that no one wanted to eat very much. By now, they must have been well out of the shipping lanes because no one said anything else about the ship that had been following them. The commander did seem to spend quite a bit of time in the radio room, though.

But no matter how stormy it was, they kept plowing south. And it wasn't long before Peter began to lose track of the days.

"How many notches do you have on your bunk, Elise?" he asked his sister one Tuesday afternoon just before they were due to report for their evening galley duty.

Elise glanced up from the game of solitaire she was playing. She had been tying small pieces of string around the end of her bunk—one piece of string for each night they had slept on board the U–111.

"Tonight will be night eleven," she replied with a forced smile.

Peter leaned over the edge of his bunk to see what Henrik was doing. His friend had just returned from a walk down the hall.

"So where do you think we are now, Henrik?"

Henrik grinned and took a breath. "Middle of the Atlantic, Mr. Andersen. And we're on the surface. Storm's over."

"Yeah, I can hear the engines, but it seems too calm for us to be up on top again."

Peter slipped out of his bunk, and he and Elise followed Henrik back toward the galley. For once, the submarine wasn't pitching and rolling. And the hatch was open again, letting in the fresh sea breeze.

"Smell that, Henrik?" asked Peter with a slight grin.

Henrik smiled and nodded. The fresh air seemed to lift his spirits, too. Elise rubbed her eyes and looked up at the late afternoon sunshine filtering down through the open hatch.

"Where's your harpoon?" asked Otto, who was standing in front of the radio room.

"Harpoon?" asked Elise. Otto nodded toward the sound man.

"Gunther says he hears dolphins all around us. They make the strangest squeaks and clicks. Sometimes you can hear them right through the hull of the ship."

Peter leaned in closer, trying to catch what the instruments were picking up. Dolphins! He had never seen one close up before. Neither had Elise or Henrik.

"You mean they're right outside?" Peter pointed to the wall, and Otto nodded.

"Maybe they think we're their leader," wondered Henrik aloud. He stepped over to the galley, picked up a big metal spoon, and tapped like a drummer on an exposed piece of the submarine's metal skin.

"Henrik," yelled Peter. "What are you doing?"

"Just trying to communicate," replied Henrik with a smile. He stopped his drumming for a moment.

"Forget that." Otto motioned for them to come, and they followed him into the Zentrale.

"Chief?" shouted Otto into the brass speaking tube that connected them with the observation platform. "Seaman Bohrmann here. Permission to come upstairs with our guests? Just for a minute?"

No one answered at first, then Peter heard a whistling sound coming back down the tube.

"All right," came the chief's distinctively nasal voice. He didn't sound too pleased. "But just for a minute."

Otto led the way up the ladder, followed by Elise, Henrik, and Peter. At least this time, thought Peter, the ladder was holding nice and still. But a big spoon from the galley almost hit Peter in the face.

"Henrik, what are you doing with that spoon in your back pocket?" Peter demanded.

"Spoon? Oh, I forgot it was there."

Once on deck, they had no trouble sighting the dolphins. Peter's heart leaped to see the ocean around them alive with fins. Some of the frisky animals were leaping right out of the water, and Peter admired the wavy cream-colored stripe on their sides. Their tops were a darker gray-blue.

"Wow," exclaimed Henrik. "Look at all of them!"

Elise started counting the members of the whirling, dancing school that surrounded the submarine. It was as if the dolphins were playing a giant game of tag—the grinning animals seemed to be having the time of their lives. "Fifteen, twenty . . . Peter, there have to be thirty or forty of them! And look at their eyes. They're looking at us!"

Elise was right. Each animal seemed to look up sideways at them with a playful, intelligent dark eye. "Like they're laughing, or smiling," replied Peter. He felt like laughing back, but one look up at the sailors on duty made him change his mind. Like the other two sailors on watch, the chief didn't seem to notice or care about the dolphins. He was studying something behind them through his binoculars.

The sea itself was a calm, bright blue, almost glassy, and incredibly beautiful. Each time a dolphin broke the surface, it created its own set of brilliant ripples. Far to their right, a brilliant sun turned the tops of the ripples into gold. And the air was filled with little puffs as the dolphins breathed out.

"You've probably never seen dolphins before," guessed Otto. "They like to follow us around, sometimes, but I think we're too slow for them. They'll be gone in a minute or two."

Peter shook his head in wonder. The long trip had almost been worth it just to see the dolphins. For this one magical moment, he could almost forget that they were prisoners on a cramped, awful-smelling German submarine. He leaned over the railing and imagined himself on their sailboat, away from these people. Far, far away. Back home, with friendly Kronborg Castle standing guard, and dolphins jumping all around them.

"Look," whispered Elise, who seemed as caught up in the sight as Peter. She pointed off to their left. "There's a mama and a little one."

About twenty feet away a darker dolphin was trailing behind, and Peter had to look closely to notice a little shadow at the mother's side. They surfaced together, breathing in harmony.

"I see them," replied Henrik, his hand on Peter's shoulder.

"Say, Wagner," said the chief to one of his sailors. He didn't lower the binoculars from his eyes. "What do you say we do a little target practice?"

Peter looked back in alarm at the three men on watch. A dark-haired sailor grinned beneath his binoculars. "Good idea, Chief. I'll call up some of the guys. We'll use the deck gun."

Just then, another gleaming gray dolphin came up for breath right beside them—almost close enough to touch. Peter was furious at the thought that any of the beautiful animals might serve as targets for the Germans.

Not if I can help it, he decided.

"Henrik," whispered Peter. "Did you catch what the chief was saying?"

"Something about the gun?"

"They're going to shoot at the dolphins."

"No!" Henrik stared up at the Germans in disbelief.

Peter nodded. "Just follow my lead."

He scanned the ocean, then leaned over close to the railing. Elise nodded her head, waiting.

"Shoo!" Peter shouted, clapping his hands. The dolphin veered away but kept an eye on them.

"Hey, kid, what are you doing?" shouted the dark-haired sailor, annoyed. But by then Henrik and Elise had joined in.

"Shoo! Yah!" hollered Henrik with a mighty stomp. Elise joined in by clapping her hands and yelling. But the dolphins didn't seem to notice until Henrik took the mixing spoon from of his back pocket and hammered the side of the submarine.

"Hey," the chief protested, but it was too late. At the sound of Henrik's annoying metal hammering, the dolphins ducked under the waves and disappeared. Peter held back a smile.

"You little brats," added the other sailor. He lowered his binoculars for a moment to look at the waters nearby, then frowned. But Peter didn't care. Elise looked at her brother and winked.

"All right, you kids," announced the chief. "Enough of that. Everyone back down below before I throw you overboard."

"Right, Chief," Otto answered. "Sorry. I didn't know they would be a problem." He glared at them.

"Well, we don't have time for that kind of foolishness, anyway," admitted the chief.

Reluctantly, Peter took a last look at the dolphins. They were barely visible far to the left of the submarine, their dark fins cutting the surface.

"Goodbye, guys," Peter whispered to the dolphins under his breath before slipping back down through the hatch.

Once below, they dragged to their places in the galley, where Helmut was clattering pans. But before they got there, they heard the submarine's engines slow, sputter, and then quit altogether. Henrik gave Peter a questioning look.

"You don't think it's the dolphins again, do you?" asked Henrik.

They peeked out into the hallway for a clue and saw the commander disappear into the sound room.

"Keep those engines off for a few minutes," he called back over his shoulder. "I want to make sure of what we're hearing."

Peter slid closer to listen in on what the commander was telling Gunther in his cubicle.

"Same one?" the commander asked.

"Absolutely," answered Gunther. "This is no school of dolphins. We slow down, he slows down. We speed up, he speeds up. We stop, he stops. He's smart, but I don't understand why he just doesn't power up and catch us. He must know how well I can detect sounds because he's trying to stay just outside my range. There's more than dolphins following us, Commander. Like I told you before—"

In the stillness, Peter heard someone clattering down the ladder in the Zentrale. Peter turned back to the galley and ran right into Henrik, who had been standing behind him.

"Someone's coming," Peter whispered to his friend as they retreated to the galley.

Now there was no mistaking the booming voice of Dr. Wolffhardt, who had obviously joined the commander and Gunther in the sound room. Peter, Elise, and Henrik strained to make out what they were saying.

"Are we still being followed?" asked Wolffhardt.

"Yes. It's been a week," the commander observed, "and no change. Gunther thinks it's huge, from the sound of its propeller. Maybe a destroyer. They definitely have our scent."

"How many?" asked Wolffhardt.

"Just one right now, but I've heard others," replied the radioman. "And beg your pardon, Commander, but Helmut told me we still have two eels left."

Peter looked over at the other two. Everyone knew that an "eel" was a torpedo. But the commander just grunted. "I guess you could call them that. I was lucky to scrape those two up before we left Kiel. But not even Helmut knows if they'll work."

"It's worth a try," said Wolffhardt. "I say we try."

"I'll make that decision," the commander snapped back. "You're always too eager to put us in danger, Wolffhardt."

"Well, I don't know if I like your decisions anymore."

There was an icy silence, then Wolffhardt continued in a softer tone. "You're trying to run this submarine with just a handful of men; no one's getting any sleep. It's easy to make mistakes under these circumstances, Karl. You look terrible. I say—"

"Don't you tell me what to do!" thundered the commander. "Remember our agreement? You take care of selling the treasure, and I'll take care of getting us to South America. Go up and count your money, but stay out of my way!"

"But we need to get them off our trail," insisted Wolffhardt. "They're obviously following us to see where we're going."

"Yes, and what if we do shoot? We only have two torpedoes. If we miss, we'll have the entire American navy on our backs. This is supposed to be a quiet cruise to South America. We'll make no waves."

"It's too late for that," snarled Wolffhardt. "If we get rid of the shadow now, quickly, no one will ever know what happened to them. Then we'll be safe the rest of the way."

With a chill, Peter turned back to their kitchen chores, peeling carrots and stirring canned beef stew. Something in the pit of his stomach told him that he wasn't going to like what was coming next. Ten minutes later, Helmut came storming into the galley.

"You kids get out of the kitchen," he ordered with a sweep of his hand.

"What did he say?" Henrik asked Elise, who was nibbling at the tip of a carrot.

"Don't ask any questions," insisted the little man. "The commander wants you to go to your bunks. Stay there until you're told otherwise. Move!"

The three had no choice but to leave their chores and follow the excited Helmut up the hallway in the direction of their sleeping quarters. One of the officers stepped out from his bunk and gave Helmut a slap on the back.

"Now's your chance to do something useful, eh, Helmut?"

"Make them swim, Helmut," said another.

Peter wasn't sure if they meant the Americans or the torpedoes. Either way, it didn't sound good. They quickly climbed up into their bunks as Helmut continued forward to the torpedo rooms with two other sailors. Behind them, they could hear the quiet hum of the E-motors jump to life and the shouts of men preparing to dive. Then the dive horn sounded, and more men ran past their bunks.

Elise looked up at Peter in desperation. "We can't just sit here and let them sink an American ship," she whispered. "Can we?"

Feeling sick, Peter shook his head. "But what can we do about it?"

"Battle stations," blared the commander's voice over the loudspeakers. From the forward compartments just ahead of their bunks came Helmut Bockstruck's excited voice, crowing instructions to his helpers.

"*Nein*, nein!" he shouted. "No! Not there. Lower it carefully into the chute. Don't bump—"

Helmut was interrupted by a voice blaring over the intercom. Wolffhardt's voice.

"Gentlemen, I want you to hear what we're up against, to give you a little boost. It's quite amusing, actually. I now bring you the voice of the American ship we're about to sink."

The loudspeakers crackled again, and a young, nervous radio voice started up faintly, then gained strength. "German submarine," came the voice. It sounded like an American reading a script written in German. "German submarine. Listen to this message. The war is over. Germany has surrendered. Surface immediately and surrender."

Wolffhardt laughed, a sinister kind of chuckle. "I told you it was amusing. Listen again."

"I repeat," came the American, pronouncing his German words slowly. "Surface immediately, and you will be returned unharmed to your country. All U-boats have been ordered by your Grand Admiral Dönitz to return to port. Surface immed—"

Wolffhardt cut off the warning speech from the American ship. "Our apologies to the grand admiral," he continued. "This will be our last assignment for the Fatherland. Or should I say, this assignment is the first one for ourselves. If we stop this ship, we should have enough time to slip away. Good luck and good hunting."

Peter had heard enough. He couldn't let it happen without at least trying something. Anything. He peeked out into the hallway to see if all was clear, then quietly slipped out of his bunk.

"Peter, what are you doing?" Elise asked him.

"We're supposed to stay in our bunks," Henrik reminded him.

"Yeah, I know," Peter whispered back. "I'm just going to check on something."

Henrik started to roll out of his bunk to follow. "Then I'm coming with you."

"Nothing doing," insisted Peter. "One person is risky enough. They'll be sure to see two."

"But what are you going to do?" Elise sounded worried.

"I'll tell you when I get back."

The idea to slip into the radio room had been growing in Peter's mind ever since Gunther had showed them the radio equipment their first day on the U-boat. Peter wasn't sure he could get anything to work, but now was the perfect time to try. He would just have to make sure that Wolffhardt was finished sharing radio blurbs with the crew.

All the crewmen seemed absorbed in their tasks. Peter had already counted four men in the torpedo rooms. He knew that usually there were at least three in the engine rooms, including Otto. That left five in the control room, including the commander, Chief Weiss, Wolffhardt, Gunther, and Dimmlich.

The only problem with his plan, Peter thought as he tiptoed up the hallway in his stocking feet, was that the radio room was practically right next to the Zentrale. If he made any noise, or if anyone happened to walk by . . .

But I can't just sit by and not try to help, he told himself. Up ahead, commands in the control room were getting louder and more intense.

"Up to periscope height," the commander barked. "Let's see what's out there."

Peter paused in the officers' wardroom, shaking at the thought of what he was trying to do. *There's still time to turn back*, he reminded himself but stuffed the thought away. *No, now's my chance.* But the commander's next question made him stop cold.

"Gunther, what do you hear out there?"

Peter froze, then ducked back out of sight next to an officer's bunk.

"They're still coming strong," reported Gunther. "Dead ahead."

"Good!" said Wolffhardt, clapping his hands. "They're not expecting us to turn around—that will be their fatal mistake. Let's circle around to the side to get a better look."

"It's risky, Wolffhardt," argued the commander. "If we miss . . ."

"But when do you ever miss, my dear commander?"

Peter must have crouched in the officer's bunk for the better part of an hour, listening to the officers argue quietly, waiting for a chance to move. But the chatter continued, getting more and more serious as they approached the ship they would attack.

"They're getting closer, Commander," said the radioman, his voice tense.

"All right, I've heard enough, Gunther," replied Commander Schulz. "We're going to need your help out here."

"Right, sir," answered Gunther.

A minute later, Peter peeked around the corner to see if the hall was clear. Satisfied but still shaking, he tiptoed once more out into the hallway, past the galley and the officers' wardroom. Finally he slipped into the empty radio cubicle. Another five steps, and he would have been in the Zentrale.

Peter huddled in the corner, breathing hard. He wished there were somewhere to hide, but the only shelter was a radio cabinet that stood out a foot from the side wall. He could wedge in behind it, but the space wouldn't necessarily hide him from view. Still, it would have to do.

Peter studied the transceiver radio Gunther had once showed them, hoping it was still set the same way it was before. If the dials and switches had been changed, how would he find the right channel to talk to the ship? Carefully, he pulled the small switch in the lower corner to the "on" position and watched the dials come to life.

As the radio warmed up, its hissing sound grew louder and louder. In panic, Peter looked for the volume to turn it down, but the hissing only intensified.

They'll hear! he worried. *Wolffhardt will come back!* Suddenly, he caught sight of a pair of earphones draped over the back of a chair. He grabbed them and quickly plugged the end into the side of the radio, cutting off the speakers.

Okay, okay, relax, Peter told himself, looking desperately from dial to dial. Behind him in the Zentrale, he could still hear Commander Schulz.

"How is it looking up forward, Helmut?" asked the Commander. "Do you have those torpedoes in place?"

"Yes, sir, almost," Peter heard Helmut answer over the intercom. "There's isn't much room up here with all of Wolffhardt's treasure."

"Just get those eels out when I tell you, Helmut," replied the commander. "We're close, now."

Peter put on the earphones, but all he could hear was static.

He was afraid to turn the tuner but couldn't think of what else to do.

This was a stupid idea, he thought. *I'm never going to get through, and the Germans will catch me.* How could he talk without someone hearing?

Without warning, a clear, American voice blasted over his earphones, loud enough to make Peter jump. He turned down the volume.

"German submarine," repeated the American, this time in English. "Surface NOW!"

Grabbing the microphone, Peter tried to pull himself into the corner behind the tall radio case. He knew what he had to do, so with one last glance at the hallway, he took a breath and squeezed the long switch on the microphone handle.

"American ship," he whispered, pulling up all the English words he knew. "American ship."

Peter paused, waiting for an answer. All he heard was static, and more shouting behind him in the Zentrale.

"Tubes one and two, stand by," ordered the commander.

"Tubes one and two, ready," replied Helmut.

"Everything okay, Helmut?" the commander double-checked.

"Far as I can tell. But where did you get these secondhand torpedoes? At a Turkish flea market?"

Still there was only static on Peter's radio line. He would have to try again.

"American ship," he tried to whisper. "American ship. Hello?"

Finally the English-speaking voice returned to the radio. "Is there someone on this frequency?" asked the voice.

"Yes, yes." Peter squeezed the switch so tightly his knuckles turned white. "You must . . . um . . . this is submarine." He struggled to find the English words. *If only this person spoke Danish!*

"Hello, is there someone on this frequency?" repeated the voice. "Repeat your message. This is the USS *Guadalcanal*. Identify yourself and repeat your message."

Peter had to try again, this time louder. He raised his voice just a notch. "Hello? This is German submarine. U-one-one-one. German submarine is . . . attacking! Torpedo. Watch out!" Peter was afraid he hadn't explained himself well enough, but that was as good as he could manage in English. They would have to understand. But all he heard in return was more static.

"Helmut!" called the commander. "Open bow caps."

"Bow caps open, sir," replied Helmut from up forward. His voice sounded like that of a kid about to open a Christmas present.

"Dimmlich, come to course one-zero," the commander barked.

"Steady on course one-zero," replied Dimmlich from the control room.

"Tubes one and two ready."

"Ready," replied Helmut. "No, wait, Commander. One is jammed! This torpedo is jammed. Wait a minute!"

Peter could hear the sudden edge of panic in their voices. He crouched in the shadows behind the radio, waiting for a reply from the ship they were about to fire on.

"Gunther," the commander finally ordered. "Run up front and see if you can help Helmut get tube number one freed up. We need both those torpedoes ready, and now!"

"Yes, sir!"

Peter hardly had time to flip off the switch and set the microphone back in its place before the radioman flashed by in the hallway. Peter buried his face in the corner, as if that would hide him when so much more of his body still showed. If Gunther stopped, he would certainly see Peter—but he just ran by.

"Gunther," bawled the commander a moment later. "We're waiting. Are you about ready up there?"

A few seconds later, Gunther's voice came back over the intercom. "Helmut says it's ready, Commander."

"Finally. Fire one and two!"

The submarine shuddered as the torpedoes left the ship—first one, followed three seconds later by the second. Peter listened for a report from the Zentrale.

"These have to be good, boys," muttered the commander. "We have nothing left to follow up with. . . ."

Seconds later, Peter heard someone stomp his foot.

"How did—" began the chief.

"Don't ask!" yelled the commander. "They acted as if they saw the torpedoes even before we shot them. Turned toward us like they knew we were coming!"

"Both misses, Commander?" asked the chief.

"Two misses!" snapped the commander. "We should have had them square in the middle, dead on, but instead we miss by a hundred meters. Now they're really after us. I should never have listened to Wolffhardt. We should have run."

He snapped the handles of the periscope together viciously. "Down scope. Dive!"

Peter hadn't thought through this part. If the torpedoes missed, the American ship would come after them with guns blazing. Their only safety now was to dive, and dive deep. And now Peter would have to sneak out of the radio room before someone came after *him.*

Peter waited until two men hurried up the hallway before slipping out of the tiny room. Once he was out, he breathed more easily, but not for long. The submarine dipped into the steepest dive he had felt yet, and Peter tumbled forward down the hall-way as if he were slipping down a playground slide headfirst. He grabbed a pipe in the galley to hang on to and met Elise coming the other way.

"What happened, Peter?" whispered Elise.

"I'm not sure," Peter whispered back. "What are you doing here?"

"Just came to see if you were okay," she replied.

"I'm fine, thanks." He looked around to make sure no one was around, then leaned forward to whisper in her face. "I tried to radio the American ship. I think I got through."

"Did they sink it?" asked Elise, her eyes wide and her voice cracking.

Peter shook his head. "No. Now the Americans are after us."

15

ATTACK!

Before Peter and Elise could make their way out of the galley, the whining roar of the American ship's propellers filled the sea around the submarine. Peter almost had to plug his ears.

A high-pitched *ping, ping* noise, even louder than the propellers, followed the roar.

"What's that?" Elise worried.

The twins had no time to wonder. There was a dull, bumping sound, followed by a deafening roar and crash that sent them flying to the floor.

The lights went out, and the entire submarine rocked from the bombs exploding outside. It seemed that everything in the kitchen was falling on top of Peter and Elise. Crates of food. Pots and pans. The officers' dishes broke and shattered as they fell, and Peter heard a scream beside him in the dark.

"Down!" shouted the commander from somewhere behind them in the Zentrale. "Get us down!"

Suddenly a leak sprang above their heads, and Peter felt a shower of water. He tried to reach out to where he thought Elise had fallen, but all he could feel were broken dishes and a crate of potatoes. Something else mixed in with the wild stew of smells—something that smelled like hot motor oil.

"Are you there, Elise?" Peter called out above the confusion. Another *bump, bump* and the sub rocked again with another explosion. This one seemed to explode high above them, though.

"I'm over here, Peter," whispered Elise, her voice sounding weak. Peter tried to get up but fell to his feet as he tripped over the dish cabinet. It had come down from the wall and had wedged in between them.

"Are you okay?" ventured Peter.

"I'm okay, but I can't see a thing."

"Me either. The American ship—I wish they knew..."

The now familiar *bump, bump* sound of the depth-charge bombs traveled through the walls, and another explosion rocked the boat.

"That one wasn't as bad," said Peter. "Maybe we're getting away." He paused for a moment. "Or maybe we're sinking."

The submarine gurgled and bubbled as it went down. It sounded as if a dozen showers had been turned on inside. The air, normally as damp as in a greenhouse, now felt as wet as a rainstorm.

"I'm getting soaked over here," said Elise. Peter heard her scuffling in the dark, trying to move out of the reach of the shower that had started in the galley. Suddenly, the lights blinked and came back on.

"Wow," sighed Peter. "I think I liked this place better when it was dark."

The kitchen was worse than he had imagined. As if a tornado had come through the submarine, everything that could have fallen from the wall was on the floor. Cold salt water poured in from a broken pipe along the ceiling, mixing with broken bins of flour to make a gooey paste that was spreading all over the mess of shattered plates littering the floor. Even worse, an oil line of some sort was leaking over three open metal containers of sugar and salt. It was hard to imagine such a total mess had been created in such a short time.

"Depth!" yelled the commander.

"One hundred meters, sir."

Another blast shook them, this one not as close. Then Helmut came charging into the galley.

"Pass me everything that floats!" he ordered. "Wooden spoons, life vests—anything!"

For a moment, Peter failed to understand what the man was asking. He hesitated.

"Now!" hissed Helmut. Another blast threw them all to their feet. Helmut jumped up and tore a wooden dish rack off the wall while Elise gathered together a handful of stirring spoons. Peter found a folding table and held it up.

"Like this?" he asked.

"Ja," replied Helmut, grabbing the table. "Keep quiet."

His arms full, Helmut hurdled down the hall toward the front of the boat. Peter had never seen him move so quickly, or so quietly.

"What's he going to do?" Elise wondered. Another blast.

Peter shrugged, but a moment later they heard the swoosh of their own torpedo tube between blasts from above. Peter and Elise sat quietly for another five minutes, then ten—all the time wincing at the fierce explosions outside their submarine and wondering if the next one would explode close enough to finish them off.

After fifteen minutes, the explosions stopped, and they looked up. Even the pinging grew fainter.

"Okay, report. What's broken?" the chief yelled. "And what's working?"

"Bulbs and fuses broken, several pipes," reported a sailor. "We lost one of the compasses. And the rudder isn't responding the way it should."

"Radios are out, too," added Gunther. "But at least the outer skin seems to be holding."

"So we're a mess," concluded Wolffhardt, "but the Americans are gone."

———————

Two hours later, they were still trying to sort out the topsy-turvy chaos everywhere in the submarine. Peter wiped his brow and looked up once more from the galley floor. It was almost nine o'clock, and no one had eaten any dinner.

"I say it was the wooden trash we shot out through the torpedo tubes that saved us," Helmut told the commander as they walked by the galley. "I shot out everything but the kitchen sink so they could see it. And the Americans fell for that old trick."

"Could be, Helmut." Commander Schulz stopped to inspect the gooey confusion on the floor. "We were lucky."

"I've never seen such a mess," Peter said to Elise, Henrik, and Otto after Helmut followed the commander down the hall. Otto had been helping them clean up the galley since he and Henrik had rejoined them. "I thought we were going to die when all those bombs were going off out there."

"This was nothing," declared Otto. He grunted as he hoisted up the fallen dish cabinet. "We've been through a lot worse. That was just a little shake-up."

Elise raised her eyebrows and swept up a pile of broken glass. "I'd hate to be around when it's worse. But what was Helmut just talking about?"

Otto smiled confidently. "The oldest trick in the book: Shoot a bunch of trash out your torpedo tube, and it floats to the top. Makes the enemy think they hit you. Then you slip away."

Elise nodded her understanding.

"But those Americans were lucky, too," continued Otto. "I still don't understand how we missed. The commander never misses that kind of shot."

Elise looked nervously at her brother, who tried to change the subject.

"What was that terrible sound we heard before the bombs

started going off?" Peter asked, holding his ears. "That *ping* sound?"

"Oh, that," replied Otto. "The Americans call it sonar. It's some kind of new device they've developed that's supposed to be able to find us under the water. But I don't think it works as well as they think it does. Not with Commander Schulz around. He's the best there is at slipping away when someone is after us. We got away, didn't we?"

Elise sighed as she tried to scoop up a pile of soggy flour paste mixed with oily goo. The smell of it made Peter's stomach turn, and he grabbed his knees for a moment.

"When are we going to surface again?" he asked, looking down at the floor.

Otto tied the cabinet to the wall with a piece of wire. "I think the commander's going to stay down as long as possible."

Peter took a breath, straightened up, and helped Elise with the flour mess. "To stay away from the American ship?"

Otto nodded and frowned. "All our radios are out. So is all the sound equipment. Blasted by the wabos. Gunther can't listen for ships anymore. We're totally blind until we get up to the top and look around. That ship could come back, be right on top of us, and we wouldn't know it."

"Can't they fix the radio?" asked Peter.

"Gunther's trying," answered Otto. "But we don't have any spare parts left. He doesn't think it's going to work."

Elise relayed the exchange to Henrik.

"Ask him about South America again," he asked her.

Otto eyed Henrik suspiciously after Elise had translated his question. "No change. We've just slowed down a little."

While Otto pulled shelves back into place and picked up pieces of broken dishes, the others finished cleaning the floor. Peter wondered why the officers insisted on using breakable dishes when everyone else used metal plates. They replaced what dishes were left on the shelves. Finally, at about ten, they were able to start fixing a late dinner.

"Yech!" sputtered Elise as she took a drink of water. "This water tastes salty."

"Well, don't use it for the coffee," said Helmut, stepping into the galley. Even though he was still officially in charge of feeding the crew, he had a way of showing up only after all the work was done.

Elise held up a coffeepot. "I'm sure I filled it with fresh—"

"Here, let *me* do it." Helmut stepped up to the sink, shoving Elise to the side. He dumped out the coffeepot full of water and refilled it from the fresh water tap. With a smirk, he passed it over to Elise.

"There you go." He poured a spot of water into a cup and tasted it. "Fresh—"

Helmut sputtered the same way Elise had. "Salt water has leaked into the fresh!"

He disappeared, mumbling something about a broken valve, and didn't return again until they had almost finished preparing a fresh pot of stew. Waterless stew.

"The fresh-water maker is broken, too," he huffed as he walked by the galley. "We have an emergency reserve for drinking that should last until we reach our destination, but we can't use it for cooking. We're going to have to make do."

"Make do!" Elise protested after Helmut had disappeared once more. She stomped her foot in disgust. "How are we going to wash?" She turned to Otto, who was just about to follow Helmut down the hallway. "Don't you people ever wash your clothes?"

Otto just shrugged and looked down at his oil-stained shirt. Even Peter knew the answer to that question. "I guess no one ever thought about it."

"What about your teeth?" she continued. "Does anyone brush their teeth, at least?"

"Uhh . . ." began Otto. "Gunther does—I think."

"You men don't even try to keep clean," replied Elise. "No showers, no scrubboards, and now no fresh water. Everything on this submarine that isn't splattered with oil is gray and dingy. All your clothes, the sheets, the tablecloths! There's just no way to get them clean."

Otto shrugged again, then waved his hand. "Ah, dirt won't hurt us any. We can make it ten more days."

Peter's ears perked up at what Otto had let slip. Only ten more days! And then South America?

16

MIDNIGHT TREASURE

Peter and Elise had gotten used to the fact that there was no difference between night and day on the U–111. The lights were always on no matter what time it was. But Henrik still tossed and turned in his bunk at night. Once or twice a night he would wake Peter with his groans. Three nights after the bomb attack, Peter woke to hear Elise mumbling softly, the way she did when she read to herself.

"What did you say, Elise?" he asked softly. The talking stopped, and Elise peeked out, surprised.

"Are you awake?"

"Yeah, I'm awake. Did you find a book, or something?"

She shook her head.

"So why are you mumbling?"

"Just writing a letter."

"Oh." He thought for a minute about mailing a letter from the middle of the Atlantic Ocean and almost smiled. "Can I read it?"

"It's to Mom and Dad."

"Come on."

"Well . . ." Elise hesitated for a minute, then crumpled up the piece of paper she had found somewhere and tossed it to Peter.

"You didn't need to ball it up. You can't send it now," he told her.

"I know. But there's no way to mail it."

"That is a problem," Peter admitted, unfolding the wrinkled paper. Elise plopped back down on her pillow with a sigh.

"Friday night, June 29, 1945," he read. The writing, in pencil, was smudged but readable.

Dear Mom and Dad,

You're not going to be able to read this, but I'm writing it anyway. Peter and I are doing okay, trying to watch out for each other. But there's only one person on this German submarine who is nice to us—a teenage boy named Otto. We're not even sure if he's truly our friend, though.

All anyone here seems to care about is the Nazi treasure. I'm so sorry we ever got mixed up in this mess. I should have stopped the boys from exploring that black boat, and we should have jumped off it right away when we heard someone coming.

I'm so sorry, Mom and Dad. You probably think we're dead. I pray every night that God will rescue us. I'm afraid . . .

The note ended with a scribble. Elise had jabbed the tip of her pencil through the paper.

"Elise, it's not your fault we're here," Peter told his sister "Really."

The submarine's engines rumbled quietly as Peter waited for Elise to reply. When she didn't, Peter tucked the note under his pillow and tried to sleep. But after a few minutes of quiet, Henrik cried out.

"It's mine," moaned Henrik. "Mine!"

"What's yours?" Peter asked quietly.

Henrik didn't answer, only moaned and rolled over.

"Peter, what's he talking about?" Elise whispered from her sleeping tent.

"Something about 'it's mine.' I don't know."

Henrik made another sound. "No!" he said, louder. "NO!"

Peter hoped no one else could hear Henrik. Anyone on the night watch would wonder at the strange conversation they were having. Peter was wide awake by now, so he hung down over the edge of his bunk to see what Henrik was doing. In the light from above, he could see his friend's angry, twisted face. Henrik's eyes seemed to be rolling behind closed eyelids, the way a dreaming person's eyes move.

"He's dreaming," Peter reported.

Henrik raised his arms, clutching something tightly in his fist. "You can't!" Henrik mumbled.

Peter looked over at Elise, who peeked out. "Should I wake him up?" he asked. He reached down to pry open Henrik's fist, only to find the gold coin.

"Look here," Peter showed the coin to Elise, and she sat up.

"He's been carrying it around," said Elise, rubbing her sleepy eyes. "I don't like it. You don't think he's going to keep the coin, do you?"

"I think he wants to," answered Peter, looking back at Henrik. "Who does it belong to anyway?"

"The government of Czechoslovakia maybe. I don't know. It sure isn't ours."

"I wish it did belong to us. It's worth a fortune. I heard Wolffhardt say so."

"Peter!" Elise snapped to attention and gave him a shocked look. "How can you say that? It's all stolen. And all these horrible men are willing to die just to have it."

Peter shook his head, embarrassed by what he had said. "Just kidding, Elise."

"You don't really want to be like them, do you? Always thinking about getting rich."

"Okay, okay. I said I was kidding. No, of course I don't want to be greedy."

He slipped out of his bunk, the gold piece warm in his hand. For another second, he let himself think of boxes full of coins—

treasures beyond what he could imagine. It was all twenty feet from his bunk. Then he shivered as he heard his grandfather's words ring through his head one more time. *"This too is meaningless, a chasing after the wind."*

Grandfather's *verse sure fits this trip,* he thought. *If this isn't chasing after the wind, I don't know what is.*

Peter put the coin into his pocket and turned down the hall. "I'm thirsty, Elise," he told his sister in a soft voice. "I'm going to get a drink."

Elise didn't reply, so he continued down the hallway. More than half the overhead lights had blown out, leaving him in shadows most of the way to the galley. Then he remembered the freshwater maker was broken. A faint voice sounded in the commander's curtained-off quarters.

"We need to stay on the surface more, that's all," the commander said, his voice drawn and quiet. He sounded even more exhausted than he had before.

"Fine," answered Wolffhardt. His voice sounded grave. "Seven more days to Belem, then up the mouth of the Amazon, where we ditch this awful tin can and meet your friend Gerlach."

"He'll be there?" asked the commander.

"I told you he would. Gerlach always keeps his word. It'll be fine."

"Fine, you say. That's what you told me before you ran into that mine and sunk your first boat. We almost lost everything there. Fine, ja."

"I recovered all the treasure, didn't I?"

"Just barely. Only after you went diving for it for a week."

"Well . . ."

"And remember how you said your friend would show up off the Dutch coast? I risked the entire mission there. And all for nothing."

"Relax, Schulz. I told you everything is going to work out just fine. Just trust me for once."

Commander Schulz sighed. "You're a fool, Wolffhardt, and

your recklessness is going to sink this ship. But I'm too tired to argue with you anymore. Now I've written everything down here—how much everyone gets, everything. We'll go over it in the morning. Right now, I'm going to check on the engine room."

Wolffhardt mumbled something else, and Peter tiptoed closer to the curtain so he could better hear what they were saying. The light snapped out, and there was a scraping of chairs, as though the men were getting to their feet. Peter quickly jumped back around the corner and hid in the galley.

Both men left the commander's quarters and disappeared toward the rear of the submarine. When Peter peeked back around the corner, no one was in sight.

Did the commander write anything about what's going to happen to us? he wondered. It would only take a second to find out.

Without making a sound, Peter slipped back to the commander's room and pushed through the curtain. Light filtered in behind him, enough so that Peter could make out a large black ledger book on the commander's writing desk. Looking quickly over his shoulder, Peter stepped up and opened it.

Expenses, fuel, radio frequencies . . . Peter leafed through the first few pages of the book and found the kinds of things he thought might be in an officer's expense book. There were duty rosters, crew lists, emergency duty assignments, diary entries. . . . He scanned down the list, seeing the familiar names. Some had notes next to them.

Excellent eyesight, the commander had written next to one of the sailor's names. *Lost his wife Gerta in 1943*, it said next to Helmut Bockstruck. Even Otto Bohrmann's name was there with a couple of penciled-in notes. *Only fifteen, but an expert diesel mechanic*, it read. *Father Max Bohrmann killed on Russian front, mother and younger brother Ludwig killed in Berlin bombing.*

Peter stared at the note once more. *Family killed.* Was this the same family Otto expected to see when they arrived in South America? The commander and Wolffhardt had been lying to Otto all along!

His heart fluttered as he scanned the pages for more notes, but there was no time. The commander would be back any minute. Peter carefully replaced the notebook where he had found it and peeked back out the curtain. All clear. Feeling like a thief, he slipped back out and padded down the hallway, back through the officers' wardroom and into the galley. He would get that drink after all.

Back at his bunk, Peter felt in his pocket for Henrik's gold coin. Suddenly, he felt a hot flash of panic. *The coin!* He felt his pocket again. *Where is it?*

He checked his right pocket, his left pocket, his shirt pockets, and his pants pockets again. It was gone!

"Elise," he whispered in the direction of his sister's bunk. "Have you seen that gold coin Henrik picked up?"

"You can't find it?" Elise mumbled.

"I was going to hold on to it so Henrik wouldn't lose it." Peter dug deeply into his right pocket in frustration—and put his finger through a small hole, a hole he hadn't noticed before. He groaned.

"What?" asked Elise.

"There's a hole in my pocket. Must have dropped it when I went to get a drink. I'm going to go back and find it."

"Don't let anyone see you."

"Don't worry. Just about everyone on the ship is asleep."

Peter slowly retraced his steps down the quiet hallway, his ears pounding. *I have to find it*, he told himself. *I have to find it before Henrik wakes up, or before someone else finds it.*

As he scanned the shadows around his feet, he wondered how he hadn't noticed losing the coin. It would have made a clinking sound when it hit the floor. And it could easily have rolled to the side and down into the cracks.

I'm never going to find it, he told himself as he neared the galley. The commander's curtain was still drawn and the light was on again, but there were no voices. Peter breathed a sigh of relief. At least Wolffhardt wasn't there.

A glint of metal caught his eye, and Peter got down on his knees to look closer. But it wasn't the coin, just the top of a bare bolt in the floor. Suddenly, a strong grip caught him by the right shoulder.

"Looking for something?" said a scratchy, familiar voice. Dr. Rudolph Wolffhardt pulled Peter by the shoulder of his shirt to his tiptoes.

"Ahh!" yelped Peter. His heart stopped beating, and he wanted to disappear. He couldn't get his mouth to work.

"You look like you've lost something, boy." Wolffhardt showed his wicked grin. "Maybe I should give you a hand. Would you like that?"

Peter didn't know whether to shake his head or nod. He tried to look down, but the man dropped him and grabbed him by the hair. Tears came to Peter's wide eyes.

"How about this?" asked Wolffhardt, holding up the missing gold coin with his left hand and shoving it in Peter's face. "Maybe this was what you were looking for? Huh?"

Peter was inches from the man's untrimmed skunk beard. Wolffhardt's eyes were wild with fury as he waited for Peter to say something.

"Where did you get it, kid? Tell me now, before I put you to bed in the torpedo tubes!"

At that moment, Peter knew Wolffhardt would gladly carry out his threat. There was no getting away from the half-crazed German.

"We . . . we—"

"Come on! Say it!"

Peter saw something move out of the corner of his eye. He tried to glance to the side, but Wolffhardt yanked his hair again—hard.

"Leave him alone!" Henrik demanded from the shadows. Wolffhardt loosened his grip for a second, and Peter shot a sideways glance at his sister and Henrik, standing in the hallway next to them.

"Oh, you have a couple of rescuers, I see." Wolffhardt spat out the words, then switched to Danish. "Now maybe I'll get some answers." He showed them the coin but kept his tight grip on Peter's hair.

"Where did you three street thieves pick this up?"

"We didn't steal anything," Elise said defensively.

"That's right," agreed Henrik. "I found it when we were on the black trawler you sank."

Wolffhardt's eyes softened a touch. "Really? We'll see about that."

He marched them back to their bunks and made them turn everything inside out—pillowcases, clothes, everything. Peter caught his breath, remembering what Otto had said Wolffhardt would do if he discovered Henrik was a Jew.

Is the necklace still there? he wondered, slipping his hand under Henrik's pillow.

Peter's hand closed around Henrik's Star of David, and for a second he hesitated. He picked it up, pretended to cough, and slipped it, chain and all, into his mouth. He looked back at the others, who were searching through Elise's bunk.

"That's the only one," Henrik insisted. "We promise. We didn't take anything else. And your treasure's all locked up anyway. We sure don't want it."

But Wolffhardt only threw down their blankets and gave them a vicious kick. "If anything else is missing . . ."

"Nothing else," repeated Henrik. "We're telling you the truth." He edged up against his pillow.

"Well, let me get one thing straight." Wolffhardt pointed a bony finger at Peter's face and gave him another wicked stare. "If *anything* else is missing, you can swim for the rest of the trip. Do I make myself clear?"

All three nodded seriously.

"Now, let me see what's over here," insisted Wolffhardt, edging toward Henrik's bunk. Peter saw his friend look nervously at the pillow as the German tore everything apart the way he had the other bunks. It took him only a minute to throw everything to the floor.

"Well, you're either telling the truth, or you've found yourself a little hiding place," Wolffhardt finally admitted. He gave them an odd half smile. "But don't forget you are here as our *guests*. I wouldn't want anything to get in the way of your *health*. Understand?"

They nodded again. Peter wished he could fit the chain with the star all the way under his tongue. And he hoped it didn't show through his cheek.

"Let me hear you say it!" Wolffhardt half shouted, half growled. They had met harsh, cruel men before. But this one was like something out of a scary fairy tale.

Peter shivered down to his bones. "I understand," he whispered, holding his hand in front of his mouth and trying not to choke on the Star of David. The others repeated the words.

"That's better," snickered Wolffhardt, stroking his striped beard. With that, he finally turned around and stalked back in the direction of the Zentrale.

Wordlessly, they straightened their bunks and crawled under the covers. When he was sure no one was around, Peter wiped off Henrik's star and dropped it down on top of him. His friend looked up and smiled.

"So that's what happened to it."

"Sorry. I kind of drooled all over it," Peter told him.

Henrik shook his head. "I'm the one who's sorry. I didn't think . . ."

But Peter just lay back in his bunk. "It's your dad's necklace—you can't lose it. But you really do need to find a better hiding place."

"Yeah, thanks. I will. Good night."

No one said anything for a few more minutes, and Peter thought the others were asleep. His heart was still beating fast. Then he heard Elise turn in her bunk.

"Peter?" she whispered.

"Hmm?" he answered, his face buried in his pillow.

"I was scared before, but now I'm really scared."

Peter was quiet. He closed his eyes and saw the furious face of Dr. Rudolph Wolffhardt. "Me too, Elise."

17

Breaking the News

The next morning, Peter, Elise, and Henrik woke up earlier than usual. The memory of Wolffhardt yanking his hair was still fresh in Peter's mind, like a nightmare he couldn't forget. From his bunk, he told Henrik and Elise in hushed tones what Wolffhardt and the commander had said the night before. And he also explained what he had read about Otto's parents in the commander's log book.

"They're both liars," said Henrik from his bunk. "What are we going to do?"

"I don't know what to do about Wolffhardt," said Elise. "But I think we should tell Otto about his parents."

"Maybe we should," agreed Peter. "But he'll never believe us."

Henrik hit the side of his bunk. "He has to!"

Peter rolled over and looked up at the ceiling. The rocking motion of the waves told him they were cruising on the surface again. He replayed everything that had happened the night before—reading the commander's log, Wolffhardt's wild look as he searched their blankets for gold coins. Peter's mind returned to the notebook. What had it said about Otto's family? Parents and brother killed?

That's it! He slipped down to the floor and grabbed Elise's arm.

"I know how we can convince Otto we're telling the truth," he told her.

Elise raised her eyebrows. "How?"

Even though it was still early, Peter saw Helmut poke his head out into the hallway and look their direction.

"Hey!" hollered Helmut. "Get down to the galley. I need some help right now."

There was nothing to do but follow the German to the galley, where they were set to work at their usual morning chores of preparing oatmeal and coffee for the crew.

"I'll tell you about my plan a little later," Peter whispered to his sister as he put a kettle of water on the stove to boil. "We just have to get Otto alone where no one can hear us."

Easier said than done, Peter reminded himself a few minutes later as he poured coffee for the commander. *Maybe we can tell Otto in the engine room—*

"Hey, watch it!" snapped Commander Schulz, pulling his cup back. It was filled to the brim, and coffee was spilling all over the tablecloth.

"Sorry!" Peter apologized and tried to mop up the mess with a cloth napkin, but only managed to slosh more hot coffee onto the commander's lap. Everyone at the table roared with laughter—except the commander, who stood up and scowled at Peter.

"Forget it!" ordered Commander Schulz. "You've done enough. Get out of here."

Otto followed Peter back to the galley with a grin on his face. "You're about the clumsiest cook we've ever had," he said. "It's a good thing they're not paying you for this trip."

Peter looked around. Helmut had disappeared somewhere, leaving Henrik to clean counters and Elise to stir oatmeal. "Listen, Otto, I have to tell you something."

"What? Is it as funny as you dumping coffee on the commander?" He poured himself a cup of coffee and turned to leave.

"No, really, Otto," put in Elise. "It's something you need to know. It's about your family."

Otto looked over his shoulder and frowned at them. "You don't know anything about my family."

"We do, too," insisted Elise. "The only thing we don't know is why we're telling you this, except that you're the only one on this submarine who's been nice to us."

"Look, if you want me to get you permission to go upstairs again, you can forget it. I've already done too many favors. The chief is already sore at me—"

"We don't want anything from you, Otto." Elise took another breath. "We just want to tell you that your parents aren't in South America like the commander has been telling you."

Otto's eyes narrowed.

"How would you know?"

"Peter saw an entry in the commander's log. He has a black notebook that lists everyone's names, and it contains little notes about each person in the crew."

"I don't believe you." Otto set down his coffee cup and stared straight at Peter. "Everyone in the crew?"

"Everyone," Peter echoed with a nod.

Otto crossed his arms. "So what about me?"

Elise swallowed hard. "Your father's name is . . . is . . ." She looked over at Peter for help.

"Max," Peter put in.

"Yes, right," she continued. "Max. He was killed on the Russian front."

Otto's eyes grew wide, but he said nothing as Elise continued.

"And your little brother's name is Ludwig. He was killed in Berlin with your mom—during the bombings. That's what was in the book. I'm . . . I'm really sorry, Otto, but—"

"You're lying!" insisted Otto, taking a step back. "You're making it up."

Elise just shook her head. "I wish we were, Otto. I'm just telling you what Peter read. It's true, all of it."

But Otto would hear none of it. His eyes filled with tears, and he shook his head violently as he backed out of the room. "You're lying," he insisted again. As he turned to go, he threw the coffee mug down with a crash and ran out through the Zentrale and back to the engine rooms.

A moment later, Helmut popped in. "What's all the noise in here? Yelling, things crashing . . ." Then he saw Peter on his knees in the corner of the galley picking up the broken pieces of the mug and mopping up the spill.

"You *again*?" growled Helmut. "I've about had it with your clumsiness. From now on you're not to touch anything except a clean-up mop and rags. Nothing breakable."

Peter nodded as Elise and Henrik came to help. "At least we tried to tell him," he whispered to his sister.

Henrik picked up a piece of the shattered mug. "Now what?"

18

CHASING THE WIND

Otto kept his distance for the next few days, and Peter wondered how he was handling the shattering news about his family. Outside, the weather seemed to get warmer and warmer every time the German sailors opened the main hatch. But there was little time for daydreaming. The commander had set extra lookouts above to check for the shadowy ship that still seemed to follow them at every step. Wolffhardt continued to keep his wild-eyed watch over the forward treasure rooms, and he and the commander argued often.

"Have you talked to Otto lately?" Henrik asked as they were getting ready for bed. It had been two days since Peter told Otto about his family. Elise now had sixteen pieces of string tied to her bunk to remind them of how long they had been on the U-boat.

"I thought we could convince him we were telling the truth," said Peter. "But he obviously still thinks it's some kind of trick."

"If he did think we were trying to trick him," put in Elise, "don't you think he would have told someone? And if he had told someone, we would have been in trouble a long time ago."

Peter considered his sister's logic for a minute and hoisted himself up onto his bunk. "Maybe you're right, Elise. Maybe he believes us and is trying to figure out a way to help us before they—"

"Before they what?" asked Henrik, sounding worried. "I still can't figure out what the crew is going to do with us. Maybe when they don't need us to fix food anymore, they'll just dump us overboard for the sharks."

"Don't say that, Henrik," Elise scolded. "That's morbid. We'll get out of this somehow."

But Henrik just threw himself down on his bunk, not listening. "I don't know if I care anymore."

"That doesn't sound like the cheerful Henrik I know," Elise tried to assure him. She looked over at Peter, who was trying to get comfortable on his bunk.

"Well, I'm fresh out of jokes," Henrik replied. "But if you have any, I'll listen."

"Do you ever pray, Henrik?" Elise finally asked. Henrik didn't answer right away, just sniffed. Peter wished he were brave enough to ask his best friend those kinds of questions.

"As a matter of fact, I did . . . once." Henrik sounded a bit defensive. "I prayed that we would find the treasure. But now I wish I would have kept my big mouth shut. What about you, Peter? Have you been praying for us? If you have, I don't think it's worked."

"How am I supposed to answer that?" asked Peter.

"I mean, if you've prayed for us to get away, it looks like the answer is no, doesn't it?" Henrik sounded depressed, like someone who had given up.

"I have been praying," Peter finally admitted, taking a deep breath. "I prayed about the treasure, too. But now I don't want any of it. I just want to go home. I don't want to be anything like Wolffhardt and the rest of the crew, just living to get rich." He wiggled around some more. "It's sad. But—hey, Henrik, would you stop kicking me?"

"I'm not kicking you," Henrik retorted.

Peter leaned over and searched between his thin sheets and the canvas bottom of his bunk. "What's this?"

He reached in under his blanket and pulled out a small cloth sack, something like a homemade lunch bag. There was a hard object inside.

"Who put this here?" asked Peter.

Elise looked over curiously. "It's not mine."

"Not mine, either," added Henrik.

Peter peeked into the sack, then quickly closed it. "I can't believe it," he whispered, looking up and down the hallway. "Is anyone else around?"

"No one," Elise assured him. "What's in the sack?"

Peter reached in again and pulled out what looked like a large toy pistol, a little bigger than a real gun and with a fat, round barrel. Almost afraid to touch it, Peter held up the black gun between two fingers as if it were a dead mouse. Henrik leaned out to get a better view and whistled.

"Wow!" whispered Elise. "What's that doing under your bed?"

Peter rummaged in the sack. "That's what I'd like to know. But wait—there's a note with it."

By that time, Henrik was leaning on Peter's bunk. "Read it," he insisted.

"Wait a minute," said Peter, unfolding the wrinkled note. He scanned it and began to translate it into Danish for Henrik.

"It's from Otto," he announced.

"I knew it!" declared Henrik. "But what does he want us to do with a gun? Blast our way out of here?"

"Henrik!" said Elise.

"It's not a real gun," said Peter.

Henrik picked up the weapon, turning it around in his hands. "It's not? Well, I guess it does look kind of like a toy. . . ."

Peter read further. "Otto says it's a signal gun with one flare left in it. 'The American ship is still following,' he says. 'Tomorrow after dinner, there will be a fire. Use it then. Maybe the ship will see you. Otherwise, Wolffhardt . . .' " Peter's voice trailed off.

"Otherwise Wolffhardt what?" asked Henrik, taking the note. He looked at it, turned it sideways, and handed it to Elise. "What's the last part say, Elise? I can't read it."

" 'Otherwise Wolffhardt' "—Elise looked up from the note— " 'otherwise Wolffhardt will not let you finish this trip. I heard him say so myself.' "

Henrik still seemed puzzled, as if he was trying to make sense out of what he had just heard. "A fire?" he asked. "How does Otto know there's going to be a fire? And how would we be able to get up on deck? No one has let us up there for days."

Peter took the flare gun and carefully wiggled the trigger. From what Otto had told them, they would have one chance— and one chance only—to make this flare gun work.

———

None of them could sleep that night, though the motion of the ship was gentle and easy. From upstairs they could smell fresh, warm breezes. Peter even thought he could pick out the faint scent of something that might be trees. Palm trees, maybe. The soft air was soothing and reassuring, but all Peter could feel was the hardness of the flare gun hidden under his pillow.

"You awake, Peter?" whispered Henrik.

"Sure, I'm awake," Peter whispered back.

"Got the flare gun?"

"Yeah."

"You sure you know how to use it?"

"I think so."

"Scared?"

"Terrified."

Henrik's bunk squeaked as he rolled over. "It was great of Otto to give us that gun. But even if we do fire it, I still don't know how this plan is going to work. Are you going to pray about it?"

"I've already started." Peter smiled. "From what I understand, this time tomorrow night, there should be a fire—I guess that will be our only chance to go upstairs and shoot a flare. I hope that mystery ship sees it."

For a minute, the only response was the steady hum of the submarine's engines. Then, "Peter?"

"Yeah, Henrik?"

"This is off the subject, but I just wanted to tell you I'm sorry for acting so snooty tonight."

"Snooty?"

"Yeah, you know, when I asked you if you ever prayed and said that your prayers must not be working. I didn't mean anything by it."

"Oh. It's okay."

Peter thought again about the gold coin and how Wolffhardt had almost torn Peter's hair out trying to find more. It almost made him ill to think about it.

Henrik cleared his throat. "Can I ask you one more thing?"

"Sure."

"Do you really not care about the treasure? Or are you just saying that?"

Peter sighed. "I don't know how to explain without sounding preachy."

"You're never preachy, Peter."

"Really?"

"Really. Not like your grandfather. I don't mean anything bad, but—"

"I know," Peter smiled. "If you asked my grandfather, I know what Bible verse he would quote you."

"He's not like you, Peter. You're always trying to hide your Bible, like you're embarrassed to have me see it."

Peter's ears burned. *That's going to change,* he told himself. *Maybe I need to be more like Grandfather, after all.*

Peter was just about to say something when the unmistakable smell of smoke made him open his eyes. He sniffed the air, not sure if it was from the engines. It stung his eyes. At the same time, a siren went off and men started to yell.

"Fire on board!" yelled one man.

Peter jerked up and almost bumped his head on a pipe.

"Do you smell that?" he asked Henrik. Both of them launched out of bed, almost falling into Elise's bunk.

"Elise, get up!" shouted Peter. "There's a fire!"

Peter's mind raced as he pulled on his pants. *It wasn't supposed to be until tomorrow night*, he told himself.

"I thought—" began Henrik

"Did we read the note wrong?" Peter asked Elise. Her eyes were wide with shock.

"I don't know."

"Let me go see what's going on," Peter volunteered. By then, the black smoke was getting thicker.

But Elise grabbed Peter's arm. "No, you don't. We're all going."

They hadn't taken more than three steps when Elise skidded to a stop and turned around. "Wait a minute," she yelled. "We forgot something!"

Two crewmen ran excitedly by them, yelling, as Elise returned.

The Zentrale was a confused swirl of thick smoke and shouting men. Three slid down the ladder from their lookout posts to help put out the fire in the engine room with portable fire extinguishers. But the smoke only seemed to worsen.

"Out of the way!" barked one of the men as he shoved Peter roughly to the side.

They found the far corner of the control room and ducked down to where the air was cleaner. *Is this Otto's fire?* Peter wondered, still confused. *But it was supposed to be tomorrow night.* The fire horn continued to blare, only a little louder than the chief's yelling.

The answer to his question came tripping through the engine room door to the Zentrale. Otto stared at them through the smoke, his eyes blazing. He glanced quickly behind him, stepped up to Peter, and pulled him to his feet.

"This is your fire," he half yelled into Peter's ear.

"Now?"

Otto nodded. "The gun?"

The flare gun! It was back in his bunk. Peter squeezed his eyes shut and pounded his fist into his hand, angry at himself for not thinking straight. He would have to run back and get it.

"Where is it?" asked Otto. His face was streaked with soot and oil, and his eyes seemed to glow red.

Elise stood and pulled the cloth sack out from behind her back. "I got it," she told them quietly. "I'll go."

Peter moved quickly, pulling the bag from her hand. "Thanks, Elise, but I need to do this."

Elise held on to the flare gun for an instant, but Peter's expression must have changed her mind. Henrik stood up, too, and Otto took him by the shoulder. "Help us put out the fire," he said, loud enough for anyone to hear. Otto dragged a confused Henrik through the door, leaving Peter and Elise alone.

"There's not much time," whispered Elise, scanning the room. Through the smoke, they could barely make out the shapes of two men on the other side, their backs to them.

Peter nodded and tucked the flare gun into his shirt, then stepped on the ladder leading up. *I just hope no one's up there,* he told himself, slipping up and out of sight.

The smoke still stung his eyes, but it thinned as he neared the top. He held his breath the last three steps, peered nervously out at the night, and stepped out.

"Hello?" Peter squeaked. The only reply was the gurgling sound of the engines from somewhere behind him and the lapping of waves. "Anyone here?"

No one answered, and he crawled the rest of the way up into the clean salt air. He looked back down at the dim light shining through the round hatch he had just crawled through; smoke was still pouring out. If anyone started up the ladder after him, he figured, he would have about ten seconds to shoot the flare.

He fumbled inside his shirt for the flare gun, his eyes adjusting to the darkness. *What if no one sees the flare?* he wondered. He glanced quickly around but saw only the bright white tops of moonlit waves. The land he thought he had smelled before was nowhere in sight.

He had rehearsed in his mind what he was going to do, but everything was happening so much sooner than he'd expected. He shook as he held the flare gun in his sweaty hands. And he couldn't decide where the American ship might be if it was still following them. *They're probably too far away*, he thought. *They'll never see it.*

Still, he pointed the gun straight over his head, squinted, and squeezed the trigger as hard as he could. He paused for a second, not sure if he had done the right thing. Nothing happened. No bang. No fireworks from the flare. Nothing.

"Oh no," Peter whispered under his breath. "All this for nothing."

There was only one flare, he reasoned, trying to think harder. *Maybe it doesn't work. Maybe it's a dud.*

Peter examined the pistol in the light of the moon. The trigger seemed stuck. And then he remembered. *The safety!*

In an instant, he flipped off the small hook that kept the trigger from being pulled by accident. Once again, Peter raised the pistol high over his head and squeezed.

"Pop!" The pistol kicked back in his hands as a sliver of red light hissed and sizzled up into the sky above the submarine. Even though the full moon made the night far from dark, the red flare looked like the brightest of fireworks high against the sky. Even the deck where he stood was washed in a red glow.

The only thing he hadn't expected was the loud *pop*. Peter looked nervously back down through the hatch. *They must have heard this*, he worried.

As the red star drifted high above, Peter wished he had more flares. And even though he knew there were no more, he squeezed the trigger until his finger hurt.

"We're here," he whispered. "We're here!"

But where was the American ship?

All too soon, the flare dipped down toward the waves, leaving the moon to shine alone. Somewhere out there was the ship. If only it had seen them!

Two minutes went by, then three. Still no one made any move to come upstairs. Peter almost made himself dizzy turning in circles, trying to see if anything—anyone—had seen them. And finally, off in the distance straight ahead, he thought he saw a small, bobbing white light. Below it, a pair of red-and-green lights began to grow. *Was it a ship?*

Then another streak of light flashed in the distance above the ship, and Peter knew something was happening. Maybe it was even an airplane. His heart began to race. At the same time, he heard the clatter of someone quickly coming up the metal ladder. He looked down at his hand. *I'm still holding the flare gun!*

Peter threw the gun out into the waves as far as he could and climbed off to the far corner of the platform by the large deck gun. The chief's voice came booming up the stairway.

"What do you mean, you thought I wanted you down here to help? Who told you that?"

Someone mumbled a reply that Peter couldn't understand. The streak of light was heading straight their way; the unmistakeable sound of an airplane engine was growing louder by the second.

"I don't care if the vice admiral himself were to tell you, I don't *ever* want you leaving your watch like that again, do you understand? If this were the real navy, I'd have your stripes. You're supposed to be the second watch officer! We can't leave ourselves unguarded. I thought you were up here with Wagner!"

"Yes, sir, but the fire—"

"Fire, nothing. It was just a lot of smoke in the engine room. I don't know where it came from, but it's already died down. Nothing to worry about."

The chief's head popped up through the hatch, then froze.

"What?" He hoisted himself up, then ducked down. "Dimm-lich! Sound the alarm! Dive!"

Peter crouched by the railing, frozen in fear. He was sure by then that someone out there had seen his flare—but he didn't know what to do about it. The dive horn went off below.

"Enemy plane!" shouted the chief, taking a quick bearing. "And a ship behind it!"

"How far?" asked the shocked sailor from below.

"Ten thousand meters. Just enough time to dive. Get down!"

At that, Peter jumped from his hiding place with a yell, trying to climb over the railing that separated him from the chief. "Wait!" he shouted. "Wait, I'm up here!"

But the chief had already begun to slam down the hatch. In the moment before it shut, Peter could hear his sister below.

"Peter's up there!" she screamed "Stop!"

But the hatch slammed shut with the heavy thud of metal on metal, and Peter heard the latches being driven into place.

"NO!" Peter cried as he fell on the hatch. He pounded with all his strength, frantic with fear. *This can't be happening!*

The pounding only hurt his fists, and air tanks hissed around him as the submarine began to sink. The hatch still didn't open.

"I'm up here! Don't you hear me? Elise! Henrik!"

Peter shouted until he was hoarse, pounded until he thought he would break his hands. He didn't care. But obviously neither did the Germans, and the hatch stayed stubbornly shut as sea-water bubbled and rose around him. The front of the submarine dipped, and Peter tumbled onto his face.

What do I do now? he asked himself as the deck below him plunged lower and lower. In a moment, he would be swimming.

There was only one thing to do, he decided as the airplane grew larger in the distance.

He stood up on the railing, trying to balance as the ship went down, waving with all his strength at the approaching airplane glittering in the moonlight.

For a moment, he thought the submarine might suck him under as it disappeared beneath the black waves. He felt the pull of the submarine's propellers a moment as he slipped off the side of the U-boat, then bobbed back to the top for air.

"Hey!" he yelled as the airplane came closer. It grew larger in the bright night sky. "Hey!" he shouted as it flew closer and closer. He tried to wave with one hand and keep afloat with the other, but it was too hard. He kicked off his heavy shoes, remembering another time he had been dumped into the ocean—the time he had gone fishing with his Uncle Morten.

Only this time everything was different. The water was much warmer; still cool, but not like the frigid waters he was used to in Denmark. And this time it was as if he were watching a movie being played right in front of him. He rode a wave up and caught sight of a ship's lights—this time surprisingly closer.

The plane was almost overhead, a husky-looking American fighter. Peter had never seen such a plane up close. He waved wildly as it buzzed right over him with a deafening roar, one hundred feet off the water.

"Down here!" he shouted.

But the plane continued past where Peter was swimming, then wheeled around in the distance for another pass. It came by from the side, this time lower. Off in the distance, Peter thought he saw something that looked like barrels tumble out from underneath the plane's wings.

Are they dropping rafts? he wondered at first.

"Hey, you missed!" he yelled. "I'm back here." More than anything, Peter wished he had another flare. The moon lit up the night, but not enough.

The barrels splashed into the water a long way from Peter, in the direction the plane and ship had come from. Nothing happened at first, but then Peter felt the sickening shock wave of an underwater explosion. The force of it slapped him on the chest, almost taking his breath away. In the distance, water reared up in a volcano-sized fountain.

That's when Peter realized this was no rescue squad. Apparently, the war hadn't ended yet out in the middle of the Atlantic Ocean. He was watching American planes sink the U–111!

"Wait!" he shouted at the top of his lungs, as if he could make the pilot hear. "Wait!"

Peter slapped at the water, crying, wishing desperately there was some way to get the pilot's attention. "MY SISTER'S DOWN THERE!" he screamed, but the plane only wheeled around for another pass. It dropped two more barrels, and Peter closed his eyes to wait for the thunderous underwater claps.

He shuddered even though he was expecting them and opened his eyes in time to see the plane banking away from the scene. In the distance, the ship had grown large in the shimmering waves. Peter could make out the huge, odd flat-top shape of an American aircraft carrier in the moonlight.

By then, a second plane was taking over the attack, and Peter tried once more to get its attention. "Go away!" he sobbed, waving. He was exhausted from treading water so long. "Don't you understand?"

He waited for the other plane to begin dropping bombs, too, and he prayed with his eyes open to the horrible scene in front of him.

"Lord, please protect Elise and Henrik," he prayed. "I didn't mean for it to happen like this. Please. I don't want them to die!"

The plane began its dive, and Peter held his breath. One more time, he gave an extra kick and waved with all the strength he had left. Even though the plane was pointed directly at him, it seemed too far way to see him.

But this plane didn't drop its bombs as the other had done. Instead, it tucked into a longer dive and continued racing straight at Peter. With a strength he thought was gone, Peter waved even higher than before, rearing out of the ocean almost to his waist.

"Hey!" he shouted. "Can't you see me? I'm right here!"

The American fighter veered to the side and dipped a wing as it roared over the top of Peter's head. Peter could see the outline of a pilot staring down at him as he kept up his waving.

With a hopeful whoop of relief, Peter looked back at the spot where the other plane had dropped its deadly cargo. As the American plane doubled back for another look, something bubbled up. For a moment, he wasn't sure, then the unmistakable conning tower of the German submarine slowly broke the surface. It came up partway, then seemed to fall back into the waves until it settled back into a crazy tilt.

"Yes!" Peter shouted, allowing himself a tired grin for the first time.

But the grin froze on his face when he noticed three men jump out onto the deck of the submarine. They were too far away to recognize. But they wasted no time in getting behind the submarine's three deck guns. They were obviously not going to give up without a fight. One of them swung around to follow the American fighter plane, then stopped when the huge shape of the aircraft carrier came into view, searchlights blazing. The contest was obviously over, and the men froze like animals caught in the headlights of an oncoming car.

As Peter watched, several more men struggled up onto the deck of the crippled submarine. Waves washed over the flat forward deck, now tilted at a steep angle to the side. They all held up their hands. Peter tried to make out his sister and Henrik, but they were still too far away.

Minutes later, three large open motorboats were racing their direction, each one carrying several marines with rifles ready. One of the motorboats followed a giant shaft of light from one of the searchlights and made a beeline for Peter. Caught in the blinding glare, Peter blinked and waved weakly.

"Not German," Peter tried to tell them as he was hauled up by the arms and pulled over the side of the motorized lifeboat. "Not German. Danish. Prisoner." Peter wasn't sure if he was using the right English words, but he tried everything he knew. A marine shouldered his rifle and kneeled next to where Peter was dripping and gasping in the bottom of the boat.

"You all right, pal?" asked the young marine in a thick Alabama drawl. Peter wasn't sure at first what the soldier was saying, but it sounded good. Peter nodded, looked up over the waist-high railing, and pointed at the stricken submarine, now bathed in the light from several searchlights. They were getting closer.

"Okay," answered Peter. "Sister. My sister and . . . and friend."

The young soldier put a blanket around Peter's shoulders and looked in the direction Peter was pointing. "You say your sister is on that sub, too, young fella?"

Peter nodded quickly and pointed again. "And friend."

"Hey, Lieutenant." The marine straightened up and looked over at the man steering their launch—a boat used for ferrying sailors to and from the aircraft carrier. "This little guy can't be more than eleven or twelve years old. Says his sister's on the sub, too."

The lieutenant shook his head in disbelief as they circled to retrieve the submarine passengers. "Gonna be interesting to hear this story."

As they closed in on the U–111, air bubbled furiously to the surface from somewhere around the back of the submarine, and it listed to its side even more. One of the submarine's sailors slipped from his perch and fell into the sea, only to be snatched out of the water by the waiting hands of an American soldier from one of the three boats that had gathered. But Peter still couldn't see Elise or Henrik.

Where are you? he wondered frantically. The submarine looked as though it was about to sink. Suddenly, Elise's blond head appeared at the top of the conning tower, and Peter sighed with relief. Henrik was right beside her, looking somber, and they climbed down the outside stairway to the deck.

"Elise!" shouted Peter. "Henrik! I'm here!"

Henrik looked up with a jerk, and Elise stared across the water at him as if he were a ghost.

"Peter—oh it's you!" She clapped her hands together and did a dance on the unsteady deck of the submarine.

In the meantime, the lieutenant on Peter's rescue boat was

counting heads. "Hey, you!" He pointed at Dimmlich as he was helped into the boat. "*Sprechen Sie Englisch?* You speak English?"

But the crewman only shrugged. He pointed to Gunther, who was standing on the deck, waiting his turn.

"Speak English?" the lieutenant repeated, pointing at the radioman. The submarine had settled so much that it was becoming hard to rescue the Germans without having them jump or fall into the water. Waves were washing at the deck, and the conning tower was sinking lower.

"Ja," answered Gunther, his eyes lowered in shame. "I speak."

"Well, where's the rest of your crew?" shouted the lieutenant. "I count ten. Don't you have thirty more?"

"Nein," replied Gunther. "That's all. Commander Schulz, he is last one. Not a full crew."

"Yeah, sure," said the American. Peter could tell the man wasn't happy with what he heard. He nodded at two of the marines who stood in the front of the boat with their rifles ready. "Johnson, Banks, I don't like this. Keep an eye peeled. There have to be more of them."

As much as he was glad to be rescued, Peter wanted to jump back in the water again to reach Elise and Henrik, now clinging to the deck. Four others, including Otto, waited to be rescued, as well. Then someone yelled from the top of the conning tower, near the main hatch.

Peter looked up. Wolffhardt and the commander were struggling on the upper deck. Wolffhardt was trying to push the commander over the railing to the deck below.

"Quitters," he shouted in German, pinning Commander Schulz to the railing. "You're all a bunch of losers! We could have been rich. But you're a disgrace to the Fatherland. Now, it's all mine."

Several of the marines below aimed their rifles at the pair, but the lieutenant waved them off. Wolffhardt angrily shoved the commander away and disappeared down into the submarine.

"Get down from there!" ordered the American lieutenant. "Down! *Nieder!*"

Commander Schulz got to his feet, replaced the peaked white commander's cap on his head, and then climbed down to join the others. By that time, the deck was fully under water; Elise and Henrik were clinging to the railing as they stood in waves that washed over their ankles. As their boat drew near, Peter and one of the Americans reached out as far as they dared.

"You're going to have to jump," Peter called out to his sister. Elise looked uncertainly down at the water that swirled between her and the rescue boat. If she jumped at the wrong time, she might be crushed. Peter knew it, too. He marked the seconds between the crashing white waves. *Four, three, two*, he counted. "Jump!"

Elise and Henrik leaped at the same time, splashing in the water next to the submarine. As they paddled the few feet between them, an explosion rumbled from somewhere inside the belly of the crippled sub, and it began to roll over on its side. Peter gasped. Wolffhardt was going down with his treasure!

The commander and two remaining German sailors jumped as the conning tower settled into the waves almost on top of them. Peter looked up to see water pouring into the main hatch. But there was no time to watch the ship die.

"Elise!" gasped Peter, leaning over to grab his sister's hand.

"Here you go," grunted the husky American who had caught hold of Henrik. A moment later, Peter fell into a heap with Elise and Henrik in the bottom of their lifeboat. Wet and exhausted— but safe.

The chief was at the rail of the lifeboat, following with wide eyes the last gurgle and bubble of the submarine. "Wolffhardt," Peter heard him whisper. "Wolffhardt, you fool."

"All right," barked the American lieutenant, revving up their engine and backing their lifeboat away from the site of the sunken submarine. Their boat held six survivors, and the others were on the other two boats nearby. "I want each prisoner checked for weapons before we turn back to the ship."

Peter had nothing to show; even his pockets were empty. But when Henrik pulled open the front of his wet, baggy sweater, everyone on the little boat stared in open-mouthed wonder.

"Henrik, how did you get those?" Peter finally managed to say. He bent down to pick up one of two glimmering, jewel-studded crowns. *The Nazi treasure!*

But Henrik only shook his head. "When the bombs started going off, the ship just came apart. Like before, only worse. Everyone was just running around, and Wolffhardt left the door to the front room open. I couldn't save everything, but I thought these crowns were the best. Maybe whoever owns them would like them back."

19

HOME IN ANY LANGUAGE

"Boy, we sure have some celebrities with us this time," said the American who brought them warm food and steaming mugs of watered-down coffee the next morning. A tall, black man, he wore a loose-fitting white sailor uniform. Peter studied the man's gleaming black shoes, then looked up to meet his smile. "I hear you three kids are in the papers back in the States."

He stood up straight and took in their questioning looks. "You understand what I'm telling you? You'll be home real soon now."

Peter thought he understood what the friendly man was saying. He liked the way the sailor smiled. And after the terror they had lived through in the cold, crowded submarine, the bright aircraft carrier they were on seemed like a palace. Even the small cafeteria they sat in seemed big enough to hold the entire U–111. And everything seemed to shine. Around them, American sailors in white or blue shirts and pants milled around tables of food, chatting and laughing. Some gave them curious stares.

"This ship's name?" Elise was curious.

"Oh, so the lady speaks English?" replied the steward, giving them another big grin.

"Just a little," she replied, shyly holding up two fingers pinched together.

"How about you boys?" said the man, looking from Peter to Henrik. They both shook their heads and grinned.

"Not very good," volunteered Peter. He looked over at Henrik and whispered in Danish. "If we got stuck on the moon, I'll bet Elise could figure out what everyone was saying."

"Isn't that the truth," replied Henrik.

"Welcome to the USS *Guadalcanal*," announced their new friend. "Finest escort carrier in the U.S. Navy."

"Guadal . . ." Elise began, pausing to smile.

"Canal," the man finished for her. "And I'm Joseph Brand, if you need anything." He pointed to himself. "Joe Brand. Just ask for me. For now, you Danish kids should just relax and get warmed up. Don't know how you got yourselves on that German sub, but we've got its crew here, and we're getting the whole crazy story out of that kid named Otto."

"Otto?" Henrik caught the name.

"Yeah, Otto. Just a kid." The steward put his hand out to show how tall Otto stood—just a bit taller than Henrik or Peter. "Friend of yours?"

"Kind of," repeated Elise. "German, but . . . but nice."

The man nodded as if he understood. Then he looked at Henrik and gently poked him in the chest.

"And you're the genuine hero, here, is that right?"

Henrik grinned and nodded. The tall, black man could have been reciting the New York City phone book, for all Henrik knew.

"That's right. The hero who saved the Nazi treasures of Europe. Crown jewels of someplace. They say they've been looking for these things all over the world, and now you show up with them in your shirt. How's it feel to be a hero?"

Henrik nodded again, picked up his plate, and smiled. "Yes, thank you."

The steward put back his head and laughed. "Your friend's right about your English, Henrik. But we'll teach you a few more words before we get back home to the States. Captain's already been on the radio to tell all your folks you're okay. Did you know that?"

"Our folks?" Elise repeated. Peter knew the word, too, but it didn't seem to make sense. The only kind of folks he knew were folk dancers.

"Yeah, your folks. Captain Rodgers gave them the message that you're okay."

Elise looked over at her brother and gave him a puzzled look. "Do you know who he's talking about?"

"Folks," repeated the sailor. "You know. You have parents, right? Mom and Dad?"

"Parents." Elise's face brightened. "Sure. Our folks."

She looked sideways at the boys. "Mom and Dad. They radioed them."

"I caught that," replied Peter.

Henrik looked at the sailor. "Mine too?"

The sailor went on. "They'll call your folks, too, Mr. Hero. Right now we're headed back to Norfolk. Those German fellas have a lot of explaining to do. You've never been to Norfolk, I don't suppose?"

"Norfolk?" Elise looked as if she was trying hard to follow along. "I don't think so. Near New York?"

"Not quite. South of that. Norfolk, Virginia. That's our home port."

"Home." Peter smiled. "Home is Denmark. Helsingor."

The steward looked closely at them.

"Now it's my turn," he laughed. "Helsing—where?"

"Helsingor," repeated Peter, pronouncing the last part of the word more carefully. *That's where we lived before we went chasing after the wind*, he thought. He grinned as he pictured their city with the red roofs and church steeples. He took another sip from his steaming mug and closed his eyes. "Home," he pronounced again. He liked the way the English word sounded on his tongue. Even more, he liked the thought of being there again soon.

EPILOGUE

During the war years between 1939 and 1945, Nazi soldiers really did steal and collect many of Europe's greatest treasures—including billions of dollars worth of paintings, historical artifacts, gold, coins, and sculptures. Things like Egyptian tomb figures. Rare books. Crown jewels. And many of the most famous paintings in the world.

Most of the loot was stored in salt mines. The mines were safe from bombing raids, and it was cool and dry inside. Perfect for storing the delicate paintings and other important treasures until the end of the war.

The German leader, Hitler, wanted to put all the treasures on display in his own art museum after the war. He wanted "his" treasure collection to become the finest in the world.

It didn't turn out the way Hitler and the Nazis had hoped. After all the trouble they took to steal and hide the treasures, nearly all of it was returned to the rightful owners in countries like Austria, France, and Czechoslovakia. Even the crown jewels of Czechoslovakia were found by American troops and returned to their rightful place. After all, none of the treasures belonged to the Nazis in the first place.

But some of the treasure did disappear. In the last days of the war, a German man named Martin Bormann took several boxes of valuable coins from one of the salt mines. They were worth a fortune. He was never seen or heard from again.